Tess had just l... someone called her name.

She turned and smiled at Ethan.

"Let me walk you to your car," he said.

Tess met his gaze and couldn't look away. Was it more than polite friendship she found there?

Ethan reached out and tucked her hair behind her ear. "I've wanted to do that since I first saw—"

Brakes squealed.

An engine roared.

"Run!" Ethan yelled as he pushed Tess behind his back.

A black van flew over the curb, hit the brakes, backed up and made for Tess once again.

She froze in the headlight beams. She couldn't breathe, couldn't think. She could only feel more fear than she'd ever known before.

Books by Ginny Aiken

Love Inspired Suspense

Mistaken for the Mob #26
Mixed up with the Mob #30
Married to the Mob #34
Danger in a Small Town #99

*Carolina Justice

GINNY AIKEN,

a former newspaper reporter, lives in Pennsylvania with her engineer husband and their three younger sons—the oldest married and flew the coop. Born in Havana, Cuba, raised in Valencia and Caracas, Venezuela, she discovered books early, and wrote her first novel at age fifteen while she trained with the Ballets de Caracas, later known as the Venezuelan National Ballet. She burned that tome when she turned a "mature" sixteen. Stints as a reporter, paralegal, choreographer, language teacher, retail salesperson, wife, mother of four boys and herder of their numerous and assorted friends—including soccer teams and the 135 members of first the Crossmen and then the Bluecoats Drum and Bugle Corps—brought her back to books in search of her sanity. She's now an author of more than twenty-eight published works and a frequent speaker at Christian women's and writer's workshops, but has yet to catch up with that elusive sanity.

Ginny Aiken

DANGER in a SMALL TOWN

Steeple
Hill®

Published by Steeple Hill Books™

STEEPLE HILL BOOKS

Steeple
Hill®

ISBN-13: 978-0-373-44289-8
ISBN-10:   0-373-44289-0

DANGER IN A SMALL TOWN

But let all who take refuge in you be glad; let them ever sing for joy. Spread your protection over them...
—*Psalms* 5:11

To two classy ladies and excellent editors,
Melissa Endlich and Emily Rodmell.

ONE

"So they kicked you out," Tess Graver said into her cell phone, her breath labored from jogging.

Uncle Gordon sputtered, "I tell ya, I'm fine. And now that I got 'em to put a cast on my leg, I'll prove it. You didn't have to quit your fancy-pants job in Charlotte just to come babysit me."

Tess slowed; she'd run close to three miles. "Let's talk about that later. I'll see you after supper, once I've showered, and then tomorrow morning I'll spring you from the hospital."

After a few more "Hmphs!" Tess's great-uncle hung up. She'd have to tell him about the thefts at Magnusson's Department Stores soon enough, but not over the cell phone while jogging. The situation at her last job had affected her more than she would have thought. She'd been under suspicion for a few weeks. Even after she was cleared of all wrongdoing, her fellow workers had withdrawn, and the odd looks had kept on coming her way.

She could no longer manage the Finer Footwear department under those conditions. Uncle Gordon's accident had given her the push to quit the job she'd once loved, and come back home—

"Oooof!"

Tess flew when a body hurtled out of the dense woods on the side of the road and crashed into her. She held her hands out to brace for the fall, then landed in a muddy patch, the ooze sliding between her fingers. "Hey, come back and help me up!"

Footsteps pounded down the road toward town.

Disgusted, Tess took stock. Nothing hurt more than what she could expect from the fall. The worst part of her predicament was the thick mud on her legs, belly, chest and hands. Fortunately, she'd kept her face up and only felt muck on her chin.

With slow, measured movements, she got to her knees. As she rose to her feet, she heard a rustling in the woods, more than the balmy, breezeless day warranted.

What was going on?

First a jerk had knocked her to the ground, and now…now she heard what sounded like a whimper. A shiver ran through her.

Should she go check? She had no idea what she might walk into.

Should she call the police? She might look like a fool if the sound came from an injured squirrel or something? Did squirrels cry?

Another whimper. More thrashing leaves.

Something was there. Maybe the guy who'd hit her had dumped a dog.

Maybe a child was hurt.

Tess couldn't just walk away. She eyed the heavy layer of vines, fallen twigs, branches and last fall's blanket of leaves.

She shivered again. "Lord? If you could somehow manage it, can you make sure there's no poison ivy or worse—a snake—in there?"

Taking a deep breath for courage, she stepped over the ground cover and parted the tall weeds, then made her way toward what sounded like a whimpering pup.

But as Tess rounded a massive tree trunk, she stopped. "Oh, no!"

A woman lay sprawled against a fallen tree, her too-thin face shiny with perspiration. As Tess watched, the slender body went into a spasm, her arms and legs twitched and sweat poured off her face.

"What's wrong—"

Tess cut off her question when a major seizure seemed to grip the stranger on the ground. She tried to remember anything and everything she'd heard about helping someone through a seizure. From the hazy, cobwebby depths of her memory, details of a college first-aid class floated up. The most important thing was to try and keep breathing passages unblocked.

Her heart pounded. *Lord, help! I need you here…now.*

Tess hurried over. "Easy," she murmured. "Let me help you."

When Tess went to roll the quaking body onto its

side, another convulsion hit, and she had to dodge the flailing limbs. Determined to help, Tess grasped a shoulder and pushed, but as thin as the woman was, she proved to be unbelievably strong.

Tess wrestled to get her on her side, but between the convulsions and the superhuman strength, she came close to calling it quits. Sweating, her breath coming in short, frightened spurts, Tess wedged herself between the stranger's back and the soggy ground to keep her from flopping onto her back again.

And then the woman quit her fight.

Tess slumped, panting, and ran the back of her hand across her eyes to clear away the sweat. Silence. She glanced at the still body propped up against her arm and leg.

"Oh, no…" She was still, completely still.

"No…no, no, *no!*"

Tess scrambled onto her knees to check for a pulse. But before she took hold of her thin wrist, the woman's body rolled onto its back, and she knew there was nothing to check. The chest didn't move.

A scream ripped from Tess's lips. Bile rushed up her throat. She froze for a moment, but the horror propelled her to her feet. She grasped at a branch to get her balance, glanced at the corpse, then put a hand over her mouth to stop the next scream.

Stepping back on trembling legs, she couldn't look away from the woman on the ground. Abstractly she noticed how her pretty hairdo hid her face.

Life ground to slow motion. Fear rushed through

Tess's limbs. Her pulse pounded in her ears, and her head spun. She realized she'd been holding her breath. Somewhere behind her, a car drove past.

A shudder racked her, followed by wave after wave of tremors. The urge to run, to hide overwhelmed her.

Despite the urgency of her instincts, Tess knew she couldn't leave. Not yet.

With a brief prayer for strength, she clutched her cell phone, forced her fingers to work and dialed 911. Her hands shook so hard she could barely hold the device to her ear. Relief flooded her when the dispatcher answered.

"Help!" she croaked.

The man on the other end asked for directions in a calm, measured voice.

"Don't know exactly," she said. "She's…I think she's dead. In the woods off Ratner Road, just a little past the old Wilder Barn. Hurry, *please!*"

The dispatcher's voice had given her something to hang on to for a couple of seconds, enough to make her realize she should wait by the road. She could flag down the cruisers as they came.

On her way out of the woods, she prayed for help to arrive soon; for God's comfort; for His wisdom for all involved.

Most of all, she prayed for more of the peace she'd felt so keenly just a few brief minutes earlier.

Ethan Rogers wiped the sweat off his forehead with the back of his hand. "It's way too hot for late May. And you're a slave driver, Art Reams."

The tall, thin pastor of Loganton Bible Church leaned against his shovel and sent Ethan a look of mock sorrow. "You wound me! I'm just doing my best to serve the Lord, and with the groundbreaking just two weeks away, we don't have the funds to hire someone to clear these weeds."

Ethan dropped the joking tone. "You are a servant, and I'm glad to help wherever I can. The new fellowship building's going to be great—especially the gym. Kids need that kind of space." He wiped the sweat from the back of his neck. "But you and I need a break. How about some of that iced tea you stash in the church fridge?"

Art dropped the shovel and held out a hand. They shook on it. As they crossed the parking lot, Ethan's phone rang. He glanced at the LCD display.

"Hey, peanut," he said to his youngest cousin. "What's up?"

"Would you stop with that peanut stuff?" He grinned when he heard her effort to muffle her response—she wasn't alone. "No one's going to listen to me if they hear you."

"What? You want me to call you Officer Lowe? Dunno if I can do that, kiddo."

"Well, you're going to have to." Her voice turned crisp, official. "I need your help. I'm out on a call, and it sounds like your specialty to me."

The disgust that had hovered in the back of his mind since the last drug bust he'd worked rushed to the fore-front. His muscles tensed, his stomach turned and his head began to pound. "Maggie…"

"I know, I know. You left all that behind when you

moved here, but Ethan, it's a death. We're a small-town department. We don't have much experience with stuff like this. You, though…all those years—I need you."

Ethan ran a hand over his face. He loved his youngest cousin like the sister he'd never had. They'd grown up close, living only two blocks apart. Over the years, he'd defended her against a bully, taught her to drive and convinced his aunt and uncle to let her go into law enforcement in spite of the danger.

He'd never been able to refuse her anything, but this came close.

Even though every fiber of his being screamed no, he said, "Where are you?"

Her sigh of relief told him she hadn't been as sure of his response as she probably should have been. "Come out west on Ratner Road. You can't miss the cruisers and the ambulance. We're in the woods, not fifty feet in."

Ethan slipped his phone into his pocket, fighting the urge to call her back and tell her no. It took all his determination to move toward his SUV.

Art placed an arm over Ethan's shoulders. "A call from Maggie that does this to you means bad news."

Ethan chuckled without humor. "My past doesn't seem ready to let me go. She's on a call, a woman's dead and she thinks it's drug related."

"It'll be hard," Art said, his voice compassionate, "but look at it from God's perspective. He had you trained, He had you gain a wealth of experience and knowledge and our Lord doesn't let things go to waste. I doubt He's done with that training of yours."

"Yeah, but I came to Loganton to get away from it all." Ethan pulled away to pace. "I had enough—more than enough. The sixteen-year-old who took his last breath in my arms did it. I can't go back to that."

Pain, nausea and a sense of failure filled him. "You can't imagine what you find when you make a bust. The wasted lives, little kids who watch mom and dad doing drugs…kids who'll live with those scars for the rest of their lives." He shuddered. "And no matter how hard you try to fight the good fight, there are more drugs on the street every day. I can't handle—"

"But God can. I know how rough the last year has been for you. I know you still struggle with the memories and the nightmares, but God is greater than all that. He'll see you through even the worst moments—if you let Him."

The battle raging in Ethan was one he'd thought he'd packed away in the cobwebs of his subconscious. Evidently, he hadn't done that good a job.

"What happened?"

Tess looked up at the petite police officer, then closed her eyes for a second. Images flew at her, fast and furious. Her heartbeat picked up steam again.

"I went for a jog," she said, her voice shaky. "On my way back, some jerk ran out of the woods and knocked me over." Tess scraped a smear of mud she'd missed on her right knee. "Then I heard a whimper in the woods. I thought the guy might have dumped a pup…" She shuddered. "But I found her instead."

The officer pulled a pencil from behind her right ear and a small pad from her breast pocket. "Did you see anyone else come out of the woods? Before you went in? Or through the trees?"

"No."

"Can you describe the man who hit you?"

Tess shook her head. "I'd been on the phone with Uncle Gordon, and I didn't notice a thing. All I remember is falling face-first into the mud. Sorry."

"And then...?"

Tess breathed deeply. "Then I went to find who or what I'd heard. As soon as I saw her, I ran to help. She was shaking—a seizure, I think." She remembered the struggle. "But she fought me...she was strong. And then...then she just quit. That's when I called 9-1-1."

"I'm glad you did." The officer smiled. "Your name...?"

With a deep breath, Tess tried to regain her composure. "Tess Graver, Gordon's niece, great-niece to be precise."

"I'm Maggie Lowe." She sat next to Tess on the scruffy grass at the edge of the road. "New in town?"

"No. I came to live with Uncle Gordon and Auntie Maude when my parents died—I was thirteen. After high school, I left for college, and then I worked in Charlotte for a few years after that. I'm back for good now, though. My uncle had an accident. He needs help, and he gave me a chance to leave a job that had become difficult."

"Did you know her?" Maggie dipped her head toward the woods.

"Never saw her before today."

The police officer put her hand on Tess's arm. "I know this is hard, but we need to go back over everything you remember. Why don't you start with your run. Any particular reason you came out this way?"

"It's beautiful. I used to run this route when I was on the cross-country team in high school. It's one of my favorite spots in town."

"And you were pushed down by a man you didn't see. Then you thought you heard a dog."

"That's right. I didn't want an abandoned puppy to die out here." Tears filled her eyes. "But instead of the pup—"

A sob caught in her throat, cutting off her words.

"It must have been hard." Maggie Lowe gave her a gentle smile.

Tess squared her shoulders. "I've never seen anything like it. All I wanted was to save a dog. But I never got around to looking for it."

"I would have done the same thing." Then the officer's gray eyes turned serious again. "I know it's rotten to make you think about it over and over again, but I need you to describe exactly what you remember when you saw her in the woods."

The officer knew her stuff. It was hard, but after a quick prayer, Tess did as she'd asked.

Speaking with the police officer made the slow-motion sensation go away. Tess had never seen anything so horrible before, and she didn't know how to process her feelings, her response. She wished there was more she could say, some way she could help, but it was too late; there was nothing further to do. At least she could give as clear a recounting as possible.

After Tess had related everything she could remember, Maggie told her she'd have to sign a statement that summarized the answers she'd given, and to expect more questions even after that. At the moment, she was free to go home. The PD knew where to find her.

With the passing of time, Tess's breath resumed its normal pace. It became even and regular again, as did her heartbeat. Her anguish, however, didn't change.

Ethan parked behind one of the PD's cruisers, careful not to block the road but also careful not to sink into the spring-damp earth on the shoulder. He didn't want to disturb any potential prints.

He got out and looked for his cousin. At first he didn't see her, but as he headed into the woods, he spotted her trademark black braid. She sat on a grassy patch next to a woman in running clothes.

"Hey, Mags," he said when he reached them.

Maggie's gray eyes lit when she saw him. "I'm so glad you're here." She stood, and the woman tried to do the same. She wobbled before Maggie wrapped an arm around her waist.

"Easy, there," his cousin said. "You've had a shock, and your body's not going to listen too well to what your head says."

"No kidding." The woman looked pale, and her voice shook.

Ethan watched, reining in his curiosity. He wanted

nothing to do with another crime scene or another overdose, but the runner tugged at something deep inside him. She wasn't small and delicate like Maggie, but she struck him as vulnerable. He hoped she hadn't been on her way to meet the woman who'd died.

With shaky fingers she smoothed a chocolate-colored wisp of hair back toward the pink stretchy thing that held her ponytail in place. She clamped her lips shut, and her hazel eyes looked huge. She held her hands fisted at her sides.

She looked about to break.

"Ethan!" Maggie said. "Where'd you space out to?"

He blinked, embarrassed. "Sorry, just thinking…" He let his words die off, knowing Maggie wouldn't prod. She knew him well. "It looks like you guys have everything under control. What did you need me for?"

"It's drugs, and it's…weird." She met his gaze. "How many overdoses have you found in the woods? We need your help."

"It's probably where she met her dealer. Looks like she couldn't wait until she got home for her fix." He glanced at the runner. "And this is…?"

"Oh! Sorry. Tess Graver, my cousin Ethan Rogers, formerly of the DEA. In Chicago. I called him for help. Had to twist his arm, but he's here now."

Ethan held out his hand.

Tess clasped his fingers. Hers trembled, and he felt an unexpected urge to comfort her. He knew how tough it was to watch someone die. And from a probable overdose… The sight of that would hit a person deep inside.

"Glad to meet you," he said. "In spite of the circumstances."

She smiled, not much of a smile, but at least she tried.

The sound of thrashing vegetation came from the woods. Ethan glanced over his shoulder and saw the EMTs carrying the gurney, a zippered body bag strapped on tight. The undergrowth was too heavy to roll the gurney.

Tess moaned.

Ethan turned, saw her falter.

She shuddered, then started to fall.

He reached out and caught her in his arms.

"Oh!" She blinked then met his gaze.

Ethan felt a sudden awareness, a strange sense of pieces falling into place, a warmth that didn't make any sense. His urge to comfort Tess took over, and he held her upright.

How could a stranger feel so right in his arms?

TWO

Tess stared up into intense blue eyes, only too aware of Ethan Rogers's strength. She couldn't help feeling comforted, protected, supported.

Very odd, since he was a stranger.

"Th-thanks," she murmured. Calling on her last reserves of strength, she placed her hands on that broad chest and pushed away. "I'm okay. It's just…" She waved toward the ambulance. "It hit me hard again to see that bag."

Ethan nodded. "It doesn't get any easier, either."

Which, she assumed, was why he wasn't an agent anymore. And he'd still come out when his cousin asked. Interesting man.

The ambulance pulled away silently, the unfortunate young woman past the need for a siren.

"Who is she?" Ethan asked.

Maggie gave a humorless chuckle. "We'd all like to know. I suppose we'll find out when we check her belongings. A couple of guys are still in there, gathering evidence."

He frowned. "You don't know her? Isn't she local?"

"Loganton might be small," Maggie said, "but not that small. I don't know everyone in town."

"Point taken." He glanced toward the woods. "Did you see anything back there? You said you thought it was drugs."

"I only took a quick look around, but I did see a syringe, and her face was a mess. Looks like meth to me."

"Meth." Ethan winced.

Even Tess knew about the horrors of methamphetamine. Newspapers and the evening news carried more stories each day—gangs, robbery, murder. Not only did meth bring crime in its wake, but it also ravaged every part of the user's body. "How awful."

Maggie flipped her notepad shut. "It's our third death in about a year. One was a vagrant. The other was a teen. There's always a greedy supplier somewhere, ready to make a buck off someone who's hurting and thinks drugs will make the pain go away."

Ethan's jaw tightened. "Where's it coming from?"

"Your guess is as good as mine," Maggie said. "We hadn't had even a hint of meth before these three deaths."

"Bad deal."

Maggie snorted. "I'll say."

Tess struggled to accept what she'd heard. "Does this mean Loganton really has a drug problem? I can't believe it. It's such a small, quiet town."

"Hey, Maggie!" the other officer yelled. "What's the deal? We gotta get to the hospital. You're not at one of those five-minute musical-chairs dating parties here, ya know."

Maggie blushed under her tan. "Gotta love him. Otherwise I might kill 'im." She turned to her partner. "He's my cousin, you goof!"

"Go ahead," Ethan said. "I'll meet you at the hospital."

"Can you make sure Tess gets home safely?"

"Of course."

Tess watched the cops get into the cruiser. Then, siren blaring, they sped off toward town.

"If you don't mind my asking, how'd you wind up in the middle of…?" Ethan waved.

"Believe it or not, all I wanted was some fresh air and a good run." Tess was surprised by how easy he was to talk to. Maybe it had something to do with the way he focused all his attention on her every word, how he nodded in agreement every so often, how he met her gaze and let his compassion show.

But by the time she finished, his smile was gone, and anger twisted his features. "Sounds like meth."

Tess bit her bottom lip and looked toward town. What could have led that woman down the path of drug abuse? She couldn't imagine seeking refuge or escape that way, no matter how tough life got. She started to ask, but when she faced Ethan again, something in his gaze held her back.

He stood statue-still, staring down the street, eyes narrowed, jaw tight. His thoughts had left Loganton for another place and time—his past, she was sure. A story lurked there somewhere, but Tess didn't have the right to pry. "Ah…I guess I'll see you later, Ethan. If you live in town, that is. It's small and…"

He didn't answer.

She wasn't surprised. She doubted he'd heard a word she'd said. The strangest urge to reach out, to comfort him came over her. But of course she didn't have that right, either, so she turned and gave him time to deal with his thoughts.

That's when she heard the other cops come out of the woods. She glanced back to see the older of the two men carrying what she thought was a tote bag. But it wasn't a tote bag after all. The most pathetic sound escaped the sack.

"Don't know anyone who wants a dog," the officer muttered to the other one at his side.

Another wail came from the bag.

It affected Tess more than she would have thought. "Is the dog okay?" she asked.

The officer turned. "Beats me. We haven't looked. We'll probably take him to the pound, now that his owner's dead."

Before she could stop to think, Tess blurted out, "I'll take him. I don't have a problem caring for him until I find him a permanent home. It's better than leaving him where he might be—"

She stopped, unable to voice the sad possibility.

At her side, Ethan chuckled.

The officers traded looks. Then the older one shrugged. "Fine with me, but we'll have to run it past the chief. If he's okay with it, then the pooch is yours."

"Not *permanently* mine, you understand." Tess reached for the tote bag. "It's just until I find him a new home."

Instead of handing her the bag, the officer put it on the ground. "Be careful," he said. "It's a mess. The owner was thinking more about her next fix than her dog. We found it sitting in the mud."

Another mournful wail escaped the carrier. Tess dropped to one knee and found the zipper's tab. Through the mesh window in the side, a pair of shiny black eyes peered out at her. The pup gave a soft yip.

Tears burned the back of her eyelids. Another victim of the drug nightmare. "Aw… You're not a bunch of girly goodies tucked into a big purse, are you?"

The eyes stared back, and the dog followed another yip with a whine.

Tess tugged at the zipper. "No lipstick or a brush or even hairspray." One by one, the plastic teeth parted. "You're a puppy dog, aren't you?"

"And you're the queen of the obvious." Ethan smiled as he knelt at her side.

Tess chuckled. "True. But I just want him to trust me, so I'll keep talking silly if it helps. He's all alone in the world now. I have to find him a home, and soon."

Ethan laughed. "He's already found a home but doesn't know it yet."

"What are you talking about?"

Ethan sat back on his heels. "Oh, the baby talk, the 'he's all alone in the world,' and the 'I have to find him a home….' He's got you right where a homeless pooch wants you."

"No. Really. I can't just walk away. That would be cruel. And I don't need a dog right now, not when I've just moved back to town and am trying to start a new business. Plus I have a relative to take care of. He's older and has health issues—you know. I don't need a dog."

The blue eyes twinkled. "How about you let the poor thing out of that fancy purse? You don't have to work so hard to justify yourself."

"That's what I'm working on." She wasn't going to touch that justifying comment.

He laughed again. "Don't blame me. You're the one falling for a dog you haven't even seen."

She shrugged. "Okay, okay. I feel sorry for him. I'm an animal lover. I couldn't turn my back on him. That's all."

"If you say so." Ethan gave her a mischievous smile, and Tess again noticed how attractive he was.

Another whine dragged her attention back to the pet carrier. Tess murmured a comforting croon while she put her hand up to the mesh window.

"Well?" Ethan asked. "Are you going to spring him?"

The last few teeth of the zipper came apart, and the flap-like door dropped to the ground. A tiny head with a sharp muzzle and pointy ears poked out—actually, one pointy ear; the other one flopped over one of the black eyes. A scrawny body covered in uneven tufts of dirt-brown fur followed, its toothpick legs taking short, stiff steps out of the carrier.

"What," Ethan asked, "is that?"

Tess could only blame her reaction on stress. Ethan's question struck her as hilarious. And the dog? Well, the poor animal was just plain pathetic.

"That, Ethan Rogers," she said between laughs, "is the ugliest dog on earth."

Then the ugliest dog on earth threw Tess a curve ball. The rotten little rat pranced up, crawled onto her lap, took four, maybe five spins, looked her in the eye, stretched out his bony body, licked her chin, and then plopped on her lap as if he'd spent every day of his life doing just that.

In that moment he stole her heart.

She was in trouble. Big-time.

And Ethan knew it.

"I told you so," the bigger rat said.

She ran a finger over that small, hard head. The mangy mess darted out his pink tongue and licked her finger. "It's temporary, Ethan. Just until I find him a forever home."

"Keep telling yourself that. Maybe someday you'll believe it."

Unfortunately, they both knew he was right. And too nice, too good-looking, too intriguing for her own good. Even if he was a stranger.

Lord? What's going on? I'm not ready for this.

She had an injured uncle to care for, a new business to get off the ground, an orphaned dog to tend to and she'd watched a woman overdose on meth. Tess wanted God to give her a quick and easy answer, but she suspected she wasn't going to get one anytime soon. She'd just have to watch herself.

Coming home was turning out to be more—*way* more—than she'd expected. Or maybe it was a case of finding more than she'd thought she'd find.

A sad dog and a striking man.

* * *

After the day she'd had, it didn't surprise Tess when she only managed to catch a nap or two that night. Her dreams kept taking her back to that horrible scene in the woods. She cried, she prayed and in the end, spent most of the night watching the shadows cast by an oak tree outside her window.

When the sun finally rose, she was an emotional mess. But she knew she had to pull herself together. Uncle Gordon expected her to pick him up by ten o'clock.

"Hey, you," Tess said as she walked into his drab-green and dingy-cream hospital room on time. "You're such a terror, they're kicking you out."

He winked. "A man's gotta do what a man's gotta do to get sprung."

She was glad to take him home. "You ready to roll, then? You're lucky they put your leg in that temporary cast. You can get around again."

A nurse pushed a wheelchair into the room. Uncle Gordon gave it a glare but didn't fight the inevitable. Instead he glanced back at Tess and said, "Do you call shuffling behind a walker getting around?"

The nurse chuckled.

Tess rolled her eyes. "I sure do. Would you rather sit in a wheelchair—like this one—and have me push you wherever you want to go?"

He scowled as they waited for the elevator. "You wouldn't have the time. You're too busy."

"Sure I'm busy, but I came home because you needed help. And a keeper. Molly and the others volunteered me for the job. They figured I didn't have anything better to do."

Getting her uncle into the car took every bit of Tess's and the nurse's attention. Once they had him settled in, they stowed away an overnight case, a balloon bouquet and all the sample-size toiletries he'd insisted on bringing home.

Tess thanked the nurse, then slid in behind the wheel. As she pulled away, Uncle Gordon let out another "Hmph!"

She slanted him a glance. "Okay. Let me have it."

His brows met over the bridge of his large nose and he shook a finger at her. "I'm not happy about you quitting your job in Charlotte."

"As you've told me a couple of times." She'd put him off long enough. She had to tell her uncle what had happened. "There were problems at Magnusson's. Someone began to steal from the registers, and only department managers had the codes to open the drawers. Because my department was hit three times, the police began to suspect me."

"Idiots!"

The anger in Uncle Gordon's gaze told her to hurry with her tale. "It's okay. They found the woman who did it. She worked for the IT department. She's in jail, but some of the people I worked with never got over their suspicions. I couldn't run the department if my employees were suspicious of me."

"Did they only hire idiots in that place?"

She smiled. Such simple support was worth everything to her. "No, they just couldn't get beyond their fears, and they didn't want to lose their jobs if I proved to be guilty sometime in the future."

"So now you're here, twiddling your thumbs, because of a bunch of fools. Now how can that make sense?"

"Now this *I've* told *you* more than a couple of times. I'm starting my own business. Please give me a chance. I'll show you what I'm doing once we're home."

He "hmphed" again, but didn't speak during the rest of the ride.

Tess parked in front of the house, reached out and patted his hand. "Trust me, Uncle Gordon, I'm much happier here at home. I didn't have anything better to do. Not in Charlotte."

"How can you be happier? You told me all you're going to be doing is staring at a little box with letters on it that'll suck the smarts right outta your brain."

"Oh, it's got pictures, too!" She hopped out and rounded the car to his side. "Computers have come a long way. Wait till you see the sweet laptop I bought for my new business. It's great!"

Tess helped him swing his legs out of the car then opened the rear door to grab the shiny new walker. That's when she noticed the flower bed under the bay window on the right side of the house. It was a mess. The rosebushes lay on their sides, and all the flowers had been trampled. "Would you look at that? What could have made that mess?"

Uncle Gordon glared. "I'm going to have to have me another talk with Rupert Anthony. That man's got himself a canine beast. And he thinks nothing of letting it roam and do its business on everybody else's property. But it's too much when the monster takes to trashing a man's roses. You won't ever see me harboring a dog. Uh-uh. Gordon Graver won't ever make a sap of himself over a bag of bones, fur, teeth and barks."

Uh-oh. Tess had a problem—another one—on her hands. Her new little bag of bones, fur, teeth and barks wasn't going to be welcomed by her uncle anytime soon. At least she'd postponed the confrontation by leaving the dog at The Pampered Pooch for grooming before going to pick up the semi-invalid at the hospital.

She reached into the backseat and grabbed Uncle Gordon's walker. A couple of twists later, she had it open and on the sidewalk. "They did teach you how to use this thing, right?"

He snorted. "A drill sergeant named Harry made me push it up and down the hospital hall about a million times. Of course, they taught me to use it. But I'm ditching it the minute I get used to this clunky old cast."

"You'll get rid of the walker when Dr. Meyer says you can," Miss Tabitha Cranston, Uncle Gordon's longtime lady-friend said as she marched down the sidewalk. "Is he giving you a hard time, Tess?"

"Nothing I can't handle." She closed the car door and followed her lovable curmudgeon up the front walk, and then helped him with the stairs. "He thinks he's tough, you know?"

"He does have his moments." Miss Tabitha's warm

hug was as welcome as always. "But we love him anyway, right, sugar?"

Tess turned the key in the lock, then pushed the door in. "I haven't met another man I'd be willing to move for."

Miss Tabitha helped ease the walker over the threshold. "There aren't many of those, are there?"

"See?" Uncle Gordon crowed. "I'm just about perfect. One of a kind."

"Oh, brother." Tess dropped his bag of hospital gear on the floor at the bottom of the steps. "I'll carry all this upstairs as soon as I make you comfortable."

"Tess," Miss Tabitha said, her voice unusually tentative. "I took the liberty of asking one of my boarders to meet us here. He's a nice, strong young man, and he can help us get Gordon upstairs. I think he needs to take another of those pain pills and go straight to bed before the pain gets too bad to bear."

"Bed!" he objected. "I've done nothing but lie in bed for three weeks! And you girls want me to go back to one? What's the point of busting out of the hospital, then?"

"The point," Miss Tabitha said, "is that someone else needs that hospital bed more than you, Gordon. All you have to do is lounge around and wait for the bone to heal. You can do that here just as well as there."

"I'm not going upstairs. I'm perfectly fine here." He pointed toward the living room. "I can sit on my own sofa just as well as lie on that bed!"

The minute he let go the walker, he swayed. The temporary cast, only two days old, wasn't meant for

walking. That one would come in about ten days, once
an X-ray revealed the progress the bones had made.

Tess grabbed his left arm, Miss Tabitha the right.

"You're not ready for the living room," Miss Tabitha
said with a shake of her head. Her alabaster braided
coronet loosened, and a stray wisp grazed her forehead.
"That's why Ethan's going to help you up those stairs.
He should be here any—"

The doorbell cut her off. She murmured something
about lunch, and Tess headed for the foyer. At the door
she smiled at Ethan Rogers. "Surprise, surprise!" she
said. "I didn't expect you to be the boarder Miss Tabitha
said she'd roped into helping us corral our wild man."

He smiled. "Hi, Tess." He stepped inside and went
straight to her great-uncle. "Mr. Graver *is* going to need
a hand with those stairs. Don't know about that corral-
ling bit, though. I'm a city boy all the way."

As the tall, muscular Ethan stood next to thin, wiry
Uncle Gordon, Tess grinned. "I doubt he'll give you
much trouble."

Uncle Gordon snorted again. "I don't tangle with the
law, girlie-girl! This guy's way outta my league. I know
when I'm beat. Let's go upstairs."

Ethan's jaw tightened. "Retired, Mr. Graver. I *used*
to work for the DEA."

Uncle Gordon jutted out his chin. "I'm still impressed."

"Don't be," Ethan said, his words as tight as his jaw.
"There's no glamour in law enforcement. Just a lot of
pain and heartbreak."

Hm…she'd been right. Definitely a story somewhere

under Ethan's many layers. But just as she'd told herself out on the roadside the day before, she didn't have the right to go digging. That didn't stop her from wondering what had led Ethan to leave the agency.

Her curiosity would have to go unsatisfied, though. They had a septuagenarian to get to bed.

To her surprise Ethan didn't leave right after he helped her settle Uncle Gordon in the middle of the old four-poster bed. Instead he followed her to the kitchen, where Miss Tabitha was making lunch.

She turned and waved toward the table when Tess and Ethan walked in. "Take a chair. The sandwiches are almost ready."

"Great!" Tess said. "I've missed your cooking."

Miss Tabitha tsk-tsked. "Oh, this isn't cooking. I told you, it's just sandwiches." Then she beamed her forest-green eyes at Tess. "Gordon's told me you left your job in Charlotte. How come?"

Tess didn't know anyone who could dodge Miss Tabitha's stare. But how was she going to tell the older woman about the thefts at Magnusson's Department Store? Especially with Ethan, a virtual stranger, sitting right here. How, for a brief time suspicion fell on her because of her position as manager of the Finer Footwear department? How could she tell Miss Tabitha that even after the culprit was found and Tess was cleared, the stigma of suspicion had dogged her every move at work?

She couldn't, so she fell back on the flip response. "I retired. I worked like crazy, and it was great for a while, but home is home. I'm back for good."

"Pshaw! You're barely out of diapers, Tess Graver. You've no more retired than I've taken up beach volleyball. What are you up to?"

Diapers? Beach volleyball? "I'm serious, Miss Tabitha. I'm done selling fancy flip-flops and sky-high heels for Magnusson's. I'm back in Loganton to stay. I'm starting a new business here."

"Tell me all about it."

BRIIING!

Saved by the phone! "Hold that thought," Tess said, and went to the phone. "Hello?"

Silence.

"Who's this?" she asked, but got no response. Then she shook her head and hung up. "Wrong number."

She returned to the table and realized both Miss Tabitha and Ethan were staring right at her. "What?" she asked.

Miss Tabitha arched a brow. "You were about to tell me about this new business of yours."

It was time to tell. "Well, I'm glad Molly and the rest of that bunch decided they couldn't get away to help Uncle Gordon. They gave me the chance to do what I really wanted but hadn't had the guts to go ahead and do."

"And that would be…?"

"I'm opening an online auction and consignment service. I'm going to make money off other people's junk."

Out the corner of her eye, Tess saw the disbelief on Ethan's face. Miss Tabitha, on the other hand, looked intrigued. Tess smiled at the lady she hoped her uncle would finally marry someday.

"It's not as crazy as it sounds," she said.

Miss Tabitha set thick sandwiches before them, then placed a pitcher of her trademark sweet tea in the center of the table. "Tell me."

After a quick prayer they ate, and Tess explained the online business phenomenon. True, it wasn't the most traditional of endeavors, but she liked the idea of finding new homes for usable items. "You know what they say," she added. "One man's trash is another's treasure."

Miss Tabitha tapped her spoon on the table. "Well, Tess, my dear. You've just snagged yourself your first client. I've got more than my fair share of junk. I can stand to unload a whole heap of it. If it'll help you and keep you here for Gordon, why, I can't think of a better fate for all those things."

Tess gaped.

The phone rang—again.

She smacked her mouth shut, then went to the phone. "Hello?"

This time, she heard breathing, faint and even, but got no response.

"Come on," she said. "I can hear you. What do you want?"

The breathing continued, and a sudden chill ran through her. This time, she couldn't drop the receiver soon enough. "I'll have to call the phone company. That's two times this happened in less than an hour. I hate prank callers. They really need to get a life."

"Prank?" Ethan asked, his voice taut, his eyes narrow and fixed on her face.

Wow! His look was colder than ice. "Mmm…yes. Silence, and then breathing. No big deal. It happens."

Ethan looked ready to object, but when he glanced at Miss Tabitha, he sat back and stared at the table. His fingers tapped out a rhythm against the wood.

Tess forced her thoughts back to their earlier conversation. "Are you really serious, Miss Tabitha? You want me to sell some items for you? What would you like me to sell first?"

A slow smile brightened Miss Tabitha's round, still-lovely face. "I've just the thing. It's bound to bring you a good commission, too. How would you like to list my collection of Victorian funerary urns?"

Ethan made a choked sound. Tess refused to look. She didn't blame him. After all…funerary urns? Ick! "Uh…what are funerary urns?"

"Well, honey, just what they sound like. They're the glass, ceramic or metal urns Victorian folks used to store the ashes of their dearly departed."

Oh, swell. She wants me to sell hundred-plus-year-old ashes. "Hm…" How did one ask diplomatically? "What exactly does one do with Victorian funerary urns?"

"Why, nothing, I suppose. They're just unique and rare collectibles. Victorians didn't cotton to the notion of cremation. They agreed with Scripture about the body being buried."

Tess knew her Scriptures just as well as the next Christian girl, but still, the thought of urns and ashes… she shuddered.

"That still doesn't tell me why you—" or anyone else "—would collect them."

Miss Tabitha gestured vaguely. "A distant relative left me a small collection—four or five—in her will. They're lovely, you know. A few years later I saw another one at an antiques auction and, well, that was that."

"And people pay for these things?" Tess asked.

Ethan made another sound, this one more like a stifled chuckle.

Miss Tabitha met Tess's gaze. "You wouldn't be thinking there's ashes in them, now would you?"

"Uh…er…no! No, no. Of course not." *Phew!*

Miss Tabitha flashed the mischievous grin that had stolen Tess's great-uncle's heart. "Good. I'm glad to hear that. At auction I've seen them go for hundreds and sometimes thousands of dollars."

Tess shook her head. There really was no accounting for taste, as the old saying went. "Okay, then. Why don't you bring me a couple? We'll start small and see how it goes from there."

"That sounds wonderful." Miss Tabitha turned to Ethan. "Would you be so kind as to bring them to Tess later on tonight? I'd like to get her up and running. This sounds like fun."

Ethan's eyes twinkled. "Be happy to."

Miss Tabitha studied him through narrowed green eyes. Long, silent moments later, she pushed her chair from the table. "I'd better be getting back home. I need to start supper for my guests."

"I'll walk you there," Ethan said.

Tess gathered her plate and glass and stood. "I'll take Uncle Gordon his sandwich when he wakes up from his nap."

Miss Tabitha crossed the room to the sink, washed her hands, dried them on a nearby kitchen towel and then headed toward the front hall, all the time chattering about the meal she planned to serve.

Tess laid an arm around Miss Tabitha's shoulders. "How many boarders do you have these days?"

"A full house—all four rooms are occupied. The Good Lord's blessed me with just the right amount of income to keep me independent all these years."

"I hope the boarders know how lucky they are. Not many landladies throw in gourmet meals as part of the rent."

"I'm glad this one does," Ethan said, smiling.

"Thank you, dear. I love to mess around in the kitchen, and it does my heart good to see folks enjoy the results."

"You do more than mess around," Tess said, "and you know it. I think you should open up a cooking school, give lessons, at the very least."

Miss Tabitha's green eyes twinkled. "Oh, who knows. Maybe someday. But I've all I can handle on my plate right now."

Tess hugged Miss Tabitha then held the door open. "I'll be waiting for the urns."

Ethan winked. "With bated breath."

Tess couldn't hold it back this time. She laughed. He joined her, and as Ethan escorted Miss Tabitha to the sidewalk, Tess couldn't squelch the tiny flicker of excitement. She liked Ethan Rogers.

"Lord? I did the right thing coming home, didn't I?" Only time would tell.

THREE

Later that evening Ethan delivered the urns as they'd agreed. He didn't stay long, saying he had to meet his cousin to go over the files on the three drug overdoses. Tess couldn't help the sense of loss every time she thought of the dead woman. It was good to know Loganton would have someone with Ethan's training and experience working on their drug-crime problem.

She murmured a silent prayer for anyone trapped by drugs, for someone to show them a better way, God's way.

After she had Uncle Gordon settled in for the night, she headed to her room with her Bible. She changed into her favorite blue T-shirt and polka-dot pajama pants, washed her face, brushed her teeth, took down her ponytail then turned off the overhead light. She clicked on the bedside lamp and curled up on top of her silky green-on-green comforter to pray.

But the image of the dead woman's dog—now her responsibility—intruded in her conversation with her Lord. She didn't want a nasty confrontation with Uncle Gordon, not over an abandoned dog. "Father, I know

I'm treading on thin ice here. Uncle Gordon's not crazy about dogs, and I've just taken one on—even though he's still at the groomer's tonight. I was too chicken to bring him home the same day Uncle Gordon left the hospital. Help me, please?"

She opened her worn and marked-up Bible then went straight to the book of Psalms. That's where she usually wound up when she needed comfort. Verse eleven in Psalm 5 leaped out at her, highlighted in yellow marker. "But let all who take refuge in you be glad; let them ever sing for joy. Spread your protection over them..."

She'd turned to these words time and time again while things at Magnusson's Department Store were in turmoil. Someone with knowledge of their security codes had been stealing from cash registers, most frequently from her department. As the manager, Tess had immediately come under scrutiny since she had the code for the register. No matter how vehemently she insisted on her innocence, until the culprit—a computer whiz from the IT department—was caught, her every move had been scrutinized.

She'd clung to that verse and the knowledge of the Apostle Paul's experiences, how he'd endured beatings and jailings and never stopped praising and trusting God. But it had been hard at times. These days she still found it difficult to trust people.

Even after the woman was arrested and Tess cleared, many of her fellow workers continued to avoid her. Work became intolerable. When her cousin Molly called about Uncle Gordon's situation, Tess jumped at the opportunity. She needed a fresh start.

She'd never expected to stumble on a dying woman while out for a jog.

After an hour or so she closed the Bible, turned the light off and again prayed for wisdom and the right words when she brought the dog home from the groomer's tomorrow. She fell asleep to the sound of a spring rain.

Ethan and his partner, Steve, had crouched across from the alley for hours. It wasn't the best neighborhood to work; it had hit on bad times years ago. Now it offered a haven to anyone with evil intent. Drug dealers had sunk the roots of their sick empires deep into the cracks of the crumbling pavement and had spread shoots like tentacles to choke off all life they found. Ethan and Steve were there to round up another purveyor of death.

The agency had been after Ernesto Moreno for a decade; the guy was slick. Ethan and Steve had been assigned to the Chicago end of the case three years before. All that work, all that danger, would finally come to fruition tonight. They were about to get their payoff. They had Moreno's jail cell ready.

Twenty minutes ago they'd heard their backup behind the rotting fence down one side of the alley.

Ethan was growing tired of waiting. He wanted Moreno now.

Then, at around two-thirty, three shadowy figures arrived near the trash bin that blocked the alley's far exit. The wait was coming to an end.

"Ready?" Steve asked.

"I've been ready for Moreno from day one."

The meticulous investigation had painted Moreno as a deadly Pied Piper. He'd led too many into the trap of coke, heroin and meth. That kind of poison was deadly, the meth particularly cheap and available to those with fewer means. This scum spent his time hanging out around schools. Oh, yeah, Ethan was ready.

He and Steve crept silently, hugging the fence, its jagged splinters snagging their clothes, their weapons drawn, all their senses on alert.

Inch by inch the partners edged close enough to hear the suspects' argument.

"You owe me!" the lanky one on the far left said in a raw whisper.

"I do not," spat the short, thin shadow farthest back. "You got all you gonna get."

"That's not what you said. You don't come through, I'll tell—"

PZZZZT! And then another PZZZZT!

A wail ripped through the silent night.

"We're in!" Steve cried.

Time blurred for the next few seconds. More shots rang out, these without benefit of a silencer. As Ethan rushed deeper into the alley, he tripped over something—someone who moaned.

Not Steve, Lord, please.

"Man down!" On his knees, Ethan reached for the victim's neck to check for a pulse. Close enough to feel the shallow puffs of breath, Ethan got a better look at the pain-stricken face. His stomach heaved. The victim was only a boy, a teen.

Ethan sucked in a harsh breath. This was his worst nightmare, everything he worked so hard to prevent. As dark as the night was, he still could see the bloom of blood on the boy's chest.

Another moan soughed out. The teen opened his eyes. "P-please..."

Sudden brilliance from a floodlight almost blinded him, but as he blinked, a man hurtled past him out of the alley. Ethan looked up and met black eyes filled with hatred. And then Moreno was gone.

"Nooooo!" Ethan sat up, panting, face drenched in tears. Over the past few weeks, the tormenting dreams had come farther apart, lasted less time, milder in their intensity. Tonight, however, he might as well have been back in Chicago, Robby Stoddard dying on his lap, his partner down with a bullet too close to his spine and Moreno getting away.

"When, Father? When will I be free of these dreams?"

A vicious bolt of lightning shocked Tess awake. Gusting wind blew a fine mist through the screened window and dampened Tess's face. The temperature had dropped at least fifteen degrees, turning her warm cocoon into a cold, soggy mess. Her heart pounded at the suddenness of the storm.

The crash of another thunderbolt got her on her feet and moving across the room to close the window. She bolted the window shut, then watched the wind thrash the branches of the oak tree outside. She willed her heart to slow down and her breathing to return to normal. To try and restore a sense of normalcy, she stripped the wet linens from her bed. She'd have to sleep on the couch downstairs until her mattress dried.

Five minutes later, in a dry nightshirt, Tess was still on edge. She'd never liked thunderstorms. She went to the dresser, straightened her hairbrush, mirror, bottle of perfume and makeup case.

Thunder crashed again and lightning streaked the dark sky outside her window. She loved the sense of safety in her cozy yellow-and-green room and didn't want to leave, but she couldn't climb into the wet bed again. Fed up with her jumpiness, she went to the bathroom for a drink before heading downstairs. But once she turned off the tap and took her first sip, she heard more running water. She put the cup down on the countertop, and went out to the hallway.

Tess paused to listen, hearing nothing but the continued battering of the rain. She waited, attentive to every creak the old home gave out. She must have imagined the sound.

A fierce gust of wind slammed against the house. Heavy raindrops beat against the slate roof and the leaded windows. Tess shivered, thankful for the shelter the sturdy house provided.

Then she heard the rushing water again, and this time there was no mistaking it. Water was running inside the house. She'd have to find where it was coming in before they suffered water damage.

In an excess of caution, she listened outside the private bathroom in Uncle Gordon's room and then started down the stairs. It sounded like a running faucet, but Tess had done the supper dishes herself. She knew she'd turned off that tap. After years of paying for her own utilities in Charlotte, she wasn't about to let water run overnight.

By the time she reached the foyer, she realized it wasn't a faucet dripping after all. What she heard was a full-fledged pour, and it came from the basement. Another buffet of wind hammered the house, the heavy rain thudding against the wood siding, crashing against the windows. The old quote, "It was a dark and stormy night" popped into her thoughts, and Tess laughed nervously.

It was silly to let a storm shake her up like this. "Get a grip," she said, her words echoing in the large kitchen.

Tess opened the basement door, flicked the switch in the stairwell and carefully made her way down the steep basement stairs. She didn't need to get hurt, too.

At the bottom of the stairs, she took a good look around. Stacks of boxes lined the walls, chairs were piled haphazardly on two tables in a corner, a collection of buckets covered Uncle Gordon's old and unused workbench and additional plastic storage containers, suitcases, and even a lawnmower took up every visible inch of space.

"Wow!" As Tess stared at the mess, another blast of wind set off the sound of running water again. And while she didn't find a flood, she did find an open window, one through which the rain poured in.

"Why would Uncle Gordon have left it open?" She didn't think it could have blown ajar during the storm, but the how didn't matter right then. She had to get it closed before the basement flooded. She climbed over a stack of boxes, then shoved three suitcases to one side. She never would have expected to find Uncle Gordon's basement so cluttered. He was more the neat-freak, organized and squeaky-clean type.

And to leave a window open…?

Then she realized that wasn't the case after all. No one had left the window open. The frame was locked, as it should have been. The glass pane, however, was broken, its jagged remains like a row of shark teeth along the wooden edge.

And, if she was right, the broken window flanked the torn-up rosebed outside. She looked for something to use to block out the rain. "That dog of Mr. Anthony's must really be something," she muttered. "First, he mangles half a dozen rosebushes, two azaleas and a border of petunias. Now, he's busted in a window…"

Armed with the blue plastic lid to a storage container near the broken window, she reached up and jammed it into place. Her guesstimate was good; it covered the opening, but she would still need tape to get it to stay.

Tess remembered the roll Uncle Gordon kept in the laundry room off the kitchen. She ran up, grabbed the shiny gray duct tape off the shelf and hurried back down. In the dimly lit cavern, she picked her way to the window again over and around the many hurdles. As she pulled out the lid to readjust it, she thought she saw a shadow move out in the yard.

Her heart sped up.

Her breathing grew shallow.

Her hands shook, and she had to fight the urge to run upstairs and dive into her bed.

As she stood frozen, scared, Tess told herself it must have been a play of the streetlight on the branches of the oak tree outside. But no matter how many times she repeated the thought, she didn't convince herself. Her impression had been one of a head, strong shoulders and legs. True, it had only lasted an instant, but she knew what she'd seen.

Would anyone believe her? Believe she'd seen someone walking out in the yard in the middle of a monsoon?

Probably not. Especially since now, a few minutes later, she was busy thinking up possible alternate scenarios. Like the unlikely oak branches.

She would only tell someone if she thought she'd be believed. The last few months at Magnusson's had left a deep scar. Tess didn't need anyone doubting her again.

Drenched, Tess made sure the plastic lid was crammed into the space as tightly as possible. Then she spread strip after strip of tape across it, and by the time she'd used almost the whole roll, the flood had been reduced to an occasional drop coursing down the wall.

"It'll have to do," she murmured, as she stepped back to admire her handiwork. It wouldn't win any beauty awards, but it worked—for the time being. She turned toward the stairs and started to make her way around the clutter again.

She put her hand on the top box to her right, slipped

her fingers into the now-open plastic container whose top covered the window, and hauled herself over the rain-sodden mess. "I'll have to call around and get a handyman to come in and replace the glass. At least Uncle Gordon won't be mucking around down here where he might slip and fall— Aaaaack!"

She lost her footing and landed on her right foot. Pain sliced up her leg. "Oh…oh…"

Gritting her teeth, Tess reached down and gingerly pulled a shard of glass from the sole of her foot. The ooze of blood told her she was in trouble. And without her phone, she'd have to crawl her way up the basement stairs, careful not to touch the wound to the dirty floor. She needed to call for help.

Inch by inch she made her bloody way across the basement. She climbed the stairs rear end first, step by step by step. Once she pushed her behind up over the last step, she breathed a sigh of relief. Now what?

Now she had to apply pressure to the wound. The bleeding was heavy. Then…?

Did she call an ambulance and scare Uncle Gordon with the siren and all the commotion? Or did she call Miss Tabitha on her private line, drag the poor dear out of bed in the middle of the night and scare the stuffing out of her?

She'd been gone from town for so long, she wasn't sure any of her former friends were still around or would remember her if they were. She'd find no help there.

The phone rang, sending a shot of relief right through her. Potential help. Then it hit her. Who would be calling in the middle of the night?

The phone rang again. Tess hopped across the room on her good foot, her bad foot dripping on the white-painted wood floor. "Hello?"

She could hear the caller's breathing on the other end, but she got no response. "I've had enough of your calls. This is a lousy time for another prank—"

"It's no prank," a harsh voice rasped. "It's a warning. I want it back."

Tess froze. Her heart pounded. The caller was clearly disguising his voice.

Lord, help! She dredged up all her courage. "What? What do you want?"

"You know." Then he hung up.

Tess stood in the brightly lit kitchen, the phone clutched to her chest. Chills ran through her. Her stomach knotted, and everything felt surreal.

She remembered the shadow and the broken window. Tess leaned sideways, and with a glance, checked the kitchen door. She breathed a relieved sigh when she saw the dead bolt in the locked position. When she straightened again, pain stabbed up her leg, and she gasped at the sight of the pool of blood from her cut foot. She needed medical attention, and soon. Should she go ahead and call 911? Was the person still outside? Had he been the one on the phone?

If she called an ambulance and the trespasser was still there, would the ambulance make him look for a place to hide until they came and took her away? Uncle Gordon would be left alone.

If instead she called Miss Tabitha for help, would the intruder overpower them both? And then…? Then what?

"Stop it!" She wasn't thinking clearly. The shadow had to have been the branches from the tree. And the caller? He must have made a mistake, dialed the wrong number, and in the dead of night, thought she was his intended target.

That was it. Nothing else made sense.

Another stab of pain shot up her leg, worse than before. She needed help. But who could she call?

Then it struck her. She knew one competent, capable person who she hoped wouldn't mind helping. Ethan would know what to do.

Relieved, but now keenly aware of the foot pain, she speed-dialed Miss Tabitha's boarding-house number and hoped whoever she woke up would forgive her.

"Hello?" Ethan asked, his voice rough, as though he hadn't used it in hours.

Thank you, Father. "Ethan? I'm sorry to wake you up, but I'm so glad you picked up the phone. It's Tess Graver. I need your help. One of our basement windows broke, probably during the storm, and when I went to cover it to block out the rain, I stepped on broken glass and hurt my foot. It's bleeding pretty badly, and I need to get to the E.R. Could you please help?"

"I'll get going as soon as we hang up."

His deep voice reassured her, and Tess pushed the memory of the shadow and the phone call out of her thoughts. "I…I think a neighbor's dog might have broken the window. Uncle Gordon says Rupert

Anthony, three doors down and across the street, got himself this monster of a dog. It looks like the animal broke loose, trashed our rosebed, and crashed into the window, too." *She hoped.*

"Some dog, that Rupert Anthony's pet."

His skepticism echoed her unease. For a moment, panic threatened, and Tess couldn't stand the thought of hanging up, of losing the connection, even if it existed only over the phone. Then she took a settling breath, closed her eyes and prayed another silent plea.

A tree branch and a wrong number, Tess. Remember?

"Fine," she said, marginally calmer. "Just hurry, please. I called because I don't want an ambulance to wake up Uncle Gordon, and I'm making a bloody mess in the kitchen."

"I'll be right there."

After a quick goodbye Tess hung up then hopped to the sink, biting down against the pain. She leaned to the right and unlocked the dead bolt. As the panic rose, she prayed. *Lord, it was the oak tree, right?*

Then, determined not to give in to the fear, Tess took a clean towel from the drawer to the left of the sink. She folded and dropped it on the floor, right by her foot. With teeth gritted, she pressed down, gasping from the pain, but aware she needed pressure to stanch the flow of blood.

Less than five minutes later, Ethan let himself in. When he saw the bloody trails across the floor, he sucked in a sharp breath. "You didn't tell me it was this bad."

"I did! I told you there was a lot of blood and I needed to get to the E.R."

"I didn't expect—" he waved toward her foot "—that."

A wave of dizziness struck her. Her good leg threatened to buckle, and Tess began to shiver. She waved toward the drawer. "You'll find more clean towels there. Help me out. We need to get going."

He crossed to the cupboard and returned, towel in hand. "That duct tape you're holding will help. Give me a minute, and I'll have you ready for our ride to the E.R."

Moments later, foot bundled up and no longer bleeding at an alarming rate, Ethan took her elbow and helped her stand. But then he stopped. "Wait!" he said. "How about your uncle? We can't leave him here alone. Let me get a friend to stay with him. Joe lives at Miss Tabitha's, too."

As they went out into the—thankfully—slowing rain, Ethan called and gave his friend directions. Then he eased Tess into his SUV. She again noticed his strength, but this time it came tempered with gentleness and care.

Tess sank into the leather seat. "Thanks for coming," she said when he sat behind the wheel.

He gave her a wry smile. "It's better than pacing the halls all night. I…have trouble sleeping sometimes."

"I'm sorry." A muscle tightened in his cheek. "Don't worry," she added. "I won't pry."

This time his look conveyed more than gratitude. Tess thought she saw admiration there, too. Warmth filled her, and for the first time since the bolt of lightning woke her up, she began to relax.

"We'll give Joe another minute or two," Ethan said. "Then it won't take us long to make it to the E.R."

The friend arrived. He and Ethan spoke briefly. As the man rounded the corner of the house, Tess glanced at Ethan. "Are you sure Uncle Gordon will be safe?"

"As sure as I can be. I've known Joe…oh, about six months now. He hasn't given me a reason to doubt him."

For the space of a second Tess thought how wonderful it would have been if someone at Magnusson's had spoken up for her like that. Her knotted shoulders eased a bit.

But then, when Ethan turned the key in the ignition, a car pulled away, its lights off.

In a flash her fear returned. Tess gasped. "He's real!"

Ethan shot her a look. "Who's real?"

"My shadow." She told him what she'd seen, what she'd hoped she'd only imagined, and then described the phone call in detail.

"If there was someone outside the window, do you really think he'd sit around this long?"

"I suppose you're right. But we have a broken window, and I did get another call."

"Didn't you think you should call Maggie? At least tell me what really happened?" Tess winced at Ethan's clipped words.

But before she could defend herself, he went on. "I'm glad I called Joe. Your uncle could have been in danger. At least Joe can call for help *if* your intruder returns."

As he spoke, Ethan drove, his hands sure on the steering wheel, his expression unreadable.

"Look," Tess said, after giving the night's events some thought. "I don't have anything that belongs to anyone, and that tree was making some pretty crazy shadows up in my room. Maybe I did imagine the shadow. I was pretty scared."

The muscle in Ethan's jaw worked. "A busted window, a threatening call and a car without lights. That doesn't sound like the bogeyman to me. I suspect someone was there."

He pulled up to the entrance to the E.R., set the brakes, ran around the SUV and helped her out of the car. "Thanks," she said, her voice tight. "I'll be fine. You don't have to wait—"

"Give me a break," Ethan snapped. "What kind of jerk would I be if I drove you here and then split?"

Tess blushed. "That's not it at all. I'm sorry I bothered you. You need to try and get some rest. You might see things in a more innocent light after a good night's sleep."

He snorted. "Here's a news flash. I won't get any rest until Maggie gets out there, we check things out and file a police report."

At the E.R., the wait was mercifully short. Tess couldn't wait to get back into bed and away from Ethan's intensity. After a number of stitches to close the wound and a megadose of antibiotics, they were ready to head back home. Ethan hadn't said a word since he'd called his cousin to give her a quick rundown of the night's events.

In the car again, Tess stole a glance at her companion. His gaze was fixed on the road ahead, his lips tight and thinned, his jaw as unyielding as if chiseled in rock. Tess doubted he'd hear her even if she yelled.

She'd suspected it, but now she knew Ethan bore emotional scars that ran deep—deeper than anything Tess could imagine, much less had ever encountered. His intense response tonight proved it. As attractive as he was on the surface, she knew she wasn't the right woman to deal with a man like him.

FOUR

After he helped Tess to the tan sofa in the Gravers' living room, Ethan drove down the still-empty streets of Loganton to Miss Tabitha's. Fingers of morning light gave the eastern horizon a rosy glow, something his life had lacked for what seemed like decades. The peaceful town wrapped its appeal around him like a warm quilt on an icy winter night.

And still he couldn't relax.

He wondered if he'd ever get used to the quiet streets. The years in Chicago had programmed him for traffic jams, high-speed chases, kids who darted in front of cars, gangs, stray bullets, drugs and death.

He was jaded. He expected trouble. And there had been trouble last night. If everything Tess had said was true.

No matter how hard she tried to deny it.

It wasn't that he thought she'd lied to him, but he was programmed to doubt everything and everyone. Too many years of dealing with the worst of humanity had left him with more scars than he cared to count. He'd thought moving to a place like Loganton would help.

And it did. When he worked with the teens at church and while he helped Miss Tabitha around the boarding house he could put distance between himself and the past.

But the dark hours of the night were no different here than there. Then Maggie had called on him to help the department find the source of the meth. He'd met Tess… And her midnight plea for help—

"Why, Lord?" He pounded the steering wheel with the heel of his hand. "Why couldn't you just let me leave it all behind?"

He'd cried out to God more times than he could count, and he knew God would keep His peace until His good time. But Ethan was exhausted. Painful memories haunted his nights, and his mind turned toward the darkness of suspicion during his days. A good night's sleep, even six hours straight, wasn't so much to hope for, to pray for. But it didn't come.

He'd continue to wait. And pray.

He had managed to nap for a couple of hours. Par for the course. The only difference between last night and the others was the reason he'd been awake. Usually nightmares put an end to any hope of sleep. Last night Tess's injury had kept him up.

As he dressed in a pair of khaki shorts and a light-blue polo shirt, Ethan thought back to what Tess had said. He didn't doubt she'd seen someone outside. Someone had broken the window, and he couldn't see how a dog could be to blame. Could the intruder have stuck around until they left for the hospital? Or was it an innocent neighbor driving away as Ethan thought. And what about that phone call?

Was it all connected?

Before he'd left Tess in the middle of the night, he'd asked her if she inadvertently might have taken something with her when she left Charlotte, something someone would care enough about to try and scare her into giving it back.

She'd looked stunned at the thought. "What do you think I had?" She shook her head. "I only owned the usual stuff. A couch, an armchair, table and chairs. And I sold everything except my clothes, my laptop, photo albums and a few collectibles. I brought nothing anyone would want—other than me."

If that was all she'd brought home with her. But was Tess telling the truth? She knew he'd been in law enforcement before his move to Loganton. She also knew he was helping Maggie with the investigation into the source of the meth. If she had something to hide, he was the last person she'd tell.

Could he trust Tess Graver?

He hoped so. From the moment he met her, he'd been attracted to her. Her fresh, girl-next-door good looks appealed to him, as did her easy smile. She'd held up fairly well after she found the overdose victim; Ethan knew plenty of rookie agents who would have tossed their cookies had they been in her place. He also admired her for coming home to care for her uncle. Her love for Gordon Graver, and Miss Tabitha, too, ran real and deep.

True, Tess said she'd come home to start an online

business, but those were notoriously short-lived, and she could have done that anywhere. Besides, Mr. Graver would have a walking cast soon enough. Was there more to Tess's return home than the obvious?

Had her run past the woods been as innocent as she said? Had she planned to meet the victim out there?

Or was he reverting to his old, suspect-everyone mode?

Only one way to know for sure. He had to get to know her better. And he'd start later that morning, when they'd agreed to meet with Maggie to file a police report. Because of Tess's cut foot, his cousin was coming to the Graver home to take Tess's statement rather than have her go down to the station.

To his surprise, for the first time in a long time, Ethan found himself looking forward to something. He couldn't wait to see Tess Graver again.

Three hours later Tess greeted him at the front door. "Good morning!"

Her smile, in spite of the strain his questions had put between them, seemed to brighten the light-filled room a notch more. He'd pushed pretty hard for answers, but she didn't seem to hold it against him.

Ethan didn't know how to deal with his response to Tess's appeal. On the one hand, she made him remember he was still alive. On the other, she made him remember the wounds he still bore from his former career. A woman like Tess needed a man who was whole.

He'd have to trust God, the God who hadn't answered his prayers for healing yet.

In His time. Ethan had heard the words a thousand times. Too bad God's time and his weren't one and the same.

When he realized Tess was staring, waiting for his response, Ethan shook himself and stepped inside. "Morning. How's your foot?"

She made a face as she hopped to the living room. "It only hurts when I walk. Imagine that."

Ethan would have helped her, but he got the feeling she'd bristle at the offer in the light of day. Tess Graver struck him as someone who preferred to stay in control.

"I see Maggie's not here yet," he said when she'd plopped on the living room couch. "I'd like to check out the basement while we wait. If that's okay."

"Sure. Just don't expect me to go with you." She winced and wiggled her bandaged foot. "Last night was more than enough for me."

"You're off the hook. Relax. I won't be long."

"Take our big flashlight with you," Tess called. "Uncle Gordon keeps it in the kitchen cupboard by the basement door. It's a dark, old basement, and the bulb in the overhead socket doesn't do much."

In the kitchen Ethan went straight to the cupboard. "Whoa! You weren't kidding. This *is* some specimen. I won't be in any risk of missing a clue." Ethan went down the stairs to the sound of her husky laughter. The cheerful sound did strange things to him deep inside, where a part of him had died on the streets of Chicago long ago. He had to watch himself around her. He could easily wind up caring too much for Tess.

And he might not have anything to offer in return.

Once down in the dark, damp basement, he flicked on the massive flashlight and beamed a column of light around the room. He picked his way over and around all kinds of junk to the broken window. Rain had puddled everywhere. Tess was going to have her hands full as soon as her foot healed. She'd have to empty the stacks of cardboard boxes before their contents mildewed and rotted. The scent of must was strong. He didn't envy her the job.

Then the broken glass had to be cleaned up. Large shards lay scattered across a five-foot radius. Smaller pieces littered the floor beneath Tess's makeshift window repair. Careful to avoid the glass, Ethan peeled off a corner of the duct tape, then lifted the plastic lid enough to check out what was left.

Nothing. Nothing much was left other than a couple of shards still clinging to the frame. But contrary to what Tess had suggested, nobody's pet pooch had broken the pane…panes—this was a recently installed, insulated, double-paned window. A good amount of effort and oomph had gone into breaking both sheets of glass.

Hardly an accident.

An ordinary burglar? Maybe. Maybe not.

But if not, why would someone target the Gravers? And then there was the phone call.

He turned off the flashlight and headed back upstairs. On his way he dialed his cousin on his cell. "Are you on your way yet?"

"Just leaving. Why?"

"I just checked out the Gravers' basement window. I have a bad feeling about this. Someone busted it in. You'll want to check for fingerprints. As far as I know, Tess's prints are the only ones you should find. Maybe Mr. Graver's, too. Don't know if you'll get any other prints, but you should try."

"How about yours? Will I find them, too?"

"Only on the plastic thing Tess used to block out the water. Not on the window itself. I know better than that, peanut."

She huffed at the nickname. "Good to see you're still on your game, old man."

He ignored the dig. "How soon can you get your guys out here? They could get lucky and find footprints outside. I know the chances are slim, thanks to the rain, but it doesn't hurt to check."

"I'll be there in five," Maggie answered. "Give my guys about twenty. See ya."

After he hung up, he took a good look around the blue-and-white kitchen. Ethan liked the blue walls, the white tile over the sink, the wood counters, white cabinets and big farm table in the middle. Tess had cleaned up the blood from the floor, so everything gleamed. Just like everything else he'd seen in the house. The Gravers' took pride in their home.

Back in the living room, Tess greeted him with a frown, laptop in hand. "What's wrong?" he asked.

She shook the computer. "I have a lemon. It crashed—and it's new! I'll have to get someone out here to fix it."

"So you haven't checked on your urns today."

"Let's not talk about that," she said with a wry grin. "What did you find?"

"Exactly what you said I would. I want to get someone out here to fix that window, but I'll wait until after Maggie's done with us."

She tucked a lock of hair behind an ear. "So what do you think? About the window."

"I don't know any dog that could have done that. Not without cutting itself pretty badly, and leaving fur and blood behind." The memory of a certain dog, if one cared to call that sad critter a dog, came to mind. "Speaking of dogs…where's your beast?"

Tess's hazel eyes grew huge. "Hush! Don't let Uncle Gordon hear you. I haven't…introduced them yet. He's at the groomer's. I'm supposed to pick him up today. And…and you see, I have to discuss with my uncle the benefits of pet adoption. I will, of course, but I don't want to bother him right now. I want him focused on his recovery. Besides, you know things have been crazy, and I haven't had the opportunity, the right time. You understand."

Ethan fought back a laugh. "You're going to try and hide the dog from him! I don't know anyone over the age of ten who'd try a stunt like that."

Her cheeks blazed red. She squared her shoulders, and her hazel eyes gleamed with green sparks. But she wouldn't meet his gaze. Instead she placed the laptop on a side table, then said, "It has nothing to do with age. It's all about not giving Uncle Gordon more to think about than his health."

Ethan smirked. "Something tells me Mr. Graver won't be happy to hear about your smuggled mutt."

Tess frowned. "I'm not going to smuggle him. I plan to bring him in the front door."

"But not while your uncle's around, right?" He arched a brow. "Isn't he the homeowner?"

She nodded, her bottom lip between her teeth.

"Then it *will* be a smuggled dog."

"This is the Graver *family* home. I'm a Graver, too."

"But you don't own the place."

"No, but I live here now."

He laughed. "And you tried to tell me the critter hadn't found a permanent home. It's going to take an act of congress to get that dog away from you."

Tess tipped up her chin. "I can have a pet if I want. So you can stop being a pain about it."

He laughed. "Oh, sure. Of course you can have a pet. I'll just stay on the lookout for the fireworks to start."

She sputtered, her cheeks pink, her eyes bright, her hair smooth and touchable—

Whoa! Not where his thoughts should go.

What had she said? Oh, yeah. In a determinedly bright tone, he said, "Let me warn you. Others before you have called me a pain, starting with my grandmother, mother, sisters and finishing with my partner—"

The teasing died in a flash of memory. Ethan turned away to spare Tess his turmoil. He didn't want this kind of thing, these…flashbacks to taint a relationship. He wanted to free himself of the pain when…*if* he found a woman he could…

Well, that didn't matter. He wasn't here to start anything with Tess. He was there because of last night's attempted break-in. Just that.

Coward. The condemning voice in the back of his mind rang with truth.

"Ethan? Are you okay?"

He dragged himself back from his thoughts and turned to Tess. Her concern made him feel even worse. The last thing he wanted was to worry her.

"Uh…yeah. I'm fine. I just…just thought of something."

He read the questions in her eyes, and had the sudden urge to tell her everything, to tell her about his partner, the bust gone bad, the years he'd fought crime only to finally realize there were more of the bad guys than good.

It stunned him. He hadn't told anyone but Art Reams, his pastor. And now…?

The doorbell rang. He always liked to see his cousin, but he didn't remember a time when the sight of her black hair and gray eyes had brought him so much relief.

"Hey, there!" he said with too much kick. "Glad you're finally here."

Maggie narrowed her eyes and quirked up one side of her mouth. "What's the deal?" She glanced at her watch, then stared again. "I only took six minutes."

Ethan's cheeks warmed up. "Ah…nothing, nothing! I just want to get this going. Something happened here last night, and it's not good. Come on. Let me show you the window." He made for the front door before Tess thought to try to join them outside—the large bandage didn't fit in a shoe, and the still-wet ground wouldn't do the cut any good. He needed distance right then.

At the side of the house Maggie took out a small digital camera and snapped a handful of photos. Then, careful not to disturb anything, she approached the window. But before she got there, she stopped.

"What size shoe do you wear?" she asked.

"Twelve wide." Ethan eyed the print. "It's not mine. That one's about a ten, and I never came out here last night or before you came."

She glanced at his feet, then shot a few more pictures. "Let me call headquarters, see if those guys can hurry over. We need a cast made, and I want it done fast."

"Good."

She gave him a crooked smile. "Oh, someone was here, all right, where no one should've been." She pointed toward the flower bed. "Take a look at the shrubs and flowers over there. Someone tore them out and threw them there. It's a break-in."

"Tess heard water pouring in last night, but she says they'd noticed the flower bed earlier in the day. I don't know when that might have happened, but I don't think it's been too long. The perp might have been scared away, then come back to find…whatever. But the print is fresh, newer than yesterday morning."

Maggie scribbled in her notepad. "Which means," she said when she flipped it closed, "that whoever ruined the garden was here at least after the rain slowed.

The print would have washed away during the worst of the storm."

"I wasn't sure I believed Tess about the shadow she says she saw last night, not until I checked out the basement this morning." His gut tightened. "We were lucky he didn't come back. I asked Joe to stay with Mr. Graver while we were at the hospital. But you know how that goes. A gun…a knife…" Ethan shrugged.

Maggie slipped pad and cell phone back into her pocket, then met his gaze. "Nothing was taken or disturbed inside, right?"

"I don't think so, but I wouldn't know." And he should have, he should have asked. But all he'd thought about was Tess's injured foot. "Ask Tess and Mr. Graver."

"When we go back inside. I want to wait until the guys get here with the casting kit. I don't want that dog you mentioned to come around and mess things up."

Less than five minutes later two other officers arrived. Ethan led Maggie to the porch and into the foyer.

"Hey!" Tess called from somewhere at the left side of the house. "I'm in the sunroom—it's my office now."

They found her wrestling with her laptop again at her desk, haloed by the sunlight pouring in through the walls of windows. She smiled, and her eyes sparkled, while lighter strands in her chocolate hair caught the golden glow of the sun. Even her yellow knit top seemed to glow. Ethan took a step toward her.

But then he sighed. He couldn't let her distract him. Since he wasn't the man who could offer Tess the kind of relationship she deserved, he didn't have the right to let anything grow between them. What he could do for her was use his professional experience to protect her from whatever was going on. It was time to focus on the break-in and figure out a few things.

Direct, focused and to the point. That's how he would handle his future encounters with Tess. "Maggie would like to ask you some questions," he said. The sooner they finished here, the sooner he could head back to the safety of Miss Tabitha's comfortable home.

Tess waved them over and pointed to the flowered settee at the far wall of the room. "I'm ready, Officer Lowe."

As soon as they sat, his cousin pulled out her notepad again. "First of all, please call me Maggie. And I'd rather we do this the way we did it the other day. Tell me everything you can remember. If I have any questions, I'll ask you when you're done."

Tess repeated what she'd told Ethan. She didn't seem to leave anything out. Didn't seem to add anything new, either. No inconsistencies. When she finished, Maggie asked the question he'd failed to ask.

"Is anything missing or damaged?"

Tess crinkled her brow, thought for a minute and then shook her head. "Aside from the flower bed and the window, nothing was touched. And even though he seems to think otherwise—" she looked at Ethan, apology in her gaze "—in the light of day, I've begun to doubt that anyone did either on purpose."

Maggie studied Tess. "Why do you say that?"

Tess smiled. "Let me show you." She hobbled to the

front door, opened it and pointed across the street to a white house with red shutters, surrounded by a scruffy-looking lawn. "That's Mr. Anthony's yard. Uncle Gordon says ever since he got his new dog, the yard's become a mess. Neighbors keep finding bits and pieces of old landscaping on their lawns. That poodle's a menace."

"A *poodle?*" Ethan asked, laughing.

Maggie shook her head. "Some poodle."

As they stared at the house, Miss Tabitha and Mr. Graver came down the hall. "There you are, Tess!" Miss Tabitha said. "I'm driving your uncle to the seniors' center for his weekly checkers match."

Tess frowned. "Are you sure you should be going out so soon, Uncle Gordon? You don't have your walking cast yet."

"Bah!" Mr. Graver answered. "I've got Tabby and this rattletrap thing. We'll be fine."

The shake he gave the walker made Ethan wonder about the elderly man's safety, if he had to rely on the wobbly support. Ethan looked to Miss Tabitha, one eyebrow arched.

His landlady smiled. "We'll be fine, dear. Maybe you can help him down the front steps. They're a little hard to maneuver."

Ethan hurried to offer the older gentleman his support. "You're going to need a ramp while you're in that cast," he said. "Six weeks is a long time to try and fight the steps."

Mr. Graver shook his head. "I'm getting myself that regular walking cast pretty soon. I'll manage until then."

So the independent streak ran in the family. Ethan smiled. "Just humor me. I'll take care of the ramp."

Mr. Graver looked ready to argue until he saw Maggie come to Ethan's side. He shot a look at Tess, then back at the cousins. "What's all the commotion? Why'd we need a cop?"

"I came to check out the broken window," Ethan said. "And I figured we should take the precaution and file a police report, so I called Maggie."

Tess's uncle laughed. "That's a good one, son." He turned to Maggie. "You better get yourself over to Rupert's and arrest that dog. You'll be doing Loganton a service."

Maggie frowned. "A dog can't be that bad."

"You don't know this dog." Mr. Graver clumped his walker to the sidewalk. "And Rupert hasn't figured out yet how to keep it inside the house. C'mon, Tabby. I'm ready to roll."

Ethan and Maggie traded looks. "Last time I checked," Ethan said, "poodles were fussy little dogs that don't do much more than bark and prance."

"You haven't met Montague," Mr. Graver said, shaking his head. "Rupert's gone soft in his old age."

Miss Tabitha unlocked her compact hybrid car, and Ethan helped Mr. Graver in.

"I suppose," Maggie said as Miss Tabitha went around the car, "there's always a chance the dog could've trampled the roses, stumbled and broken the window. Maybe Mr. Anthony made the footprint retrieving his pet."

Ethan snorted. "Just like it's conceivable the earth's flat."

Tess rolled her eyes. "All we have to do is ask Mr. Anthony."

"I'm on my way," Maggie said. "It won't take me but a minute to check out this dog."

Miss Tabitha started the car. Ethan and Tess waved.

"Hang on, there, Tabby!" Mr. Graver called. "I want to watch this."

Ethan fought the urge to follow his cousin. He was curious about Rupert Anthony and Montague, but more than that, he wanted to get away from Tess's appeal. By now, though, he knew Tess would insist on hobbling over, and not just her but Mr. Graver as well. He couldn't run the risk of either of them getting hurt again.

Maggie rapped on the red door. It opened, and a burly white-haired gentleman stepped out onto the front stoop. Then pandemonium broke out.

Sharp barks rang out.

The man yelled.

Maggie screamed, "Stop!"

The biggest, most ridiculous excuse for a dog Ethan had ever seen pranced into his line of sight. Yeah, more ridiculous than the plug-ugly one Tess took in.

Montague was a poodle, all right. But he was a full-size animal, at least three feet tall. His curly hair was cut in the pompoms and poufs of the breed, and he seemed determined to deafen everyone in Loganton as he took off down the steps.

Mr. Anthony chased the dog down to the next-door

yard and snapped a leash on its collar. Maggie followed. As they marched homeward, owner berated pet.

Maggie ran back. "It wasn't the poodle," she said, out of breath. "He is trouble, but he hasn't been around for five days. He's been at the vet's. Some kind of intestinal problem, Mr. Anthony said."

Ethan hoped the dog's problems were over. The Gravers, on the other hand, still had a problem, a pressing one. And it had nothing to do with the dog.

"Can you have a patrol check the house regularly?" he asked. "At least until you catch the intruder. Oh, and go ahead and tap the phones. We want to trace the caller."

"The caller!" Mr. Graver cried.

Tess took a step back, blushing, guilt on her face. "Uh…there's some more stuff I need to tell you."

Mr. Graver hmphed. "I'll say."

FIVE

Two days later, Tess sat at her desk, her laptop repaired again by a technician named Stan. She suspected she and Stan would have a long relationship—not necessarily by choice.

She was checking on her auction items. She'd listed Miss Tabitha's first urn for a short, three-day sale after she'd seen other dealers do that. From outside her window, the steady bang of hammers kept her company.

Ethan had shown up early yesterday with his buddy, Joe Medina, a Mexican immigrant in his late twenties. Joe was short and slender, with intelligent brown eyes and an unruly shock of straight black hair. Ethan introduced them right away, since the night Joe had come to stay with Uncle Gordon Tess had been in no condition for an introduction.

Ethan and Joe had become friends soon after Ethan had moved into Miss Tabitha's. They'd often joined forces to tackle the odd maintenance project for their landlady, saving her a good bit of cash, and now the Gravers would benefit from their expertise.

Tess had watched the men for a while. They'd taken measurements, scribbled notes, laughed and joked a good bit, worked much more, and by late afternoon the basement sported another new window.

Uncle Gordon had supervised every move the younger men made from the vantage point of a chair they'd set up for him under the oak. The only thing that got his goat was the extra cost of having to replace a less than one-year-old window.

If it weren't for the memory of the phone calls, of that harsh whisper on the other end of the connection, and the reality of the attempted break-in, Tess would have been happy, content with the choices she'd made. She loved being home, and she also loved watching the interest generated by the few things she'd put up for sale.

Yesterday she'd taken photos of two more urns Miss Tabitha wanted sold, the microwave she'd brought home with her and no longer needed and a collection of quirky key chains Uncle Gordon didn't want. Today she was uploading the lot, posting her rules and regulations and choosing closing dates for each of her sales.

"Knock, knock!" Ethan called from the doorway to the sunroom. "I see your laptop's healthy again. How's the online auction business going?"

"The technician came out right away." She turned to her laptop, clicked on an icon or two, then pointed at the screen. "Want to take a look at my listings?"

"As long as you have something besides funerary urns for sale."

She laughed. "I don't have much that might interest you

right now. But I'm sure once people in Loganton figure out what I'm doing I'll have stock with broader appeal."

"So it's just the urns."

"And a few things I don't need, now that I'm home. Can I interest you in a microwave? It's practically brand-new. I bought it about two weeks before I decided to move back."

He gave her a smug smile. "I have no use for a microwave. *I* get to enjoy Miss Tabitha's cooking every day."

"Now that's a treat."

"She's better than many of Chicago's chefs."

"Is that where you used to work?"

"Yes," he said.

The temperature in the sunroom plunged about fifty degrees with her mention of his former job. The awkwardness shot up to the clouds.

Great. Now what?

"Um…well, I'm loving my work." How could she get them back to where they'd been? Ethan seemed miles away.

Tess studied his handsome features, marred by a frown and stonelike jaw. It wasn't anger she saw, but rather pain, and the urge to comfort him overcame her as it had in the woods that other day.

She had to admit, she really did like Ethan Rogers. She especially admired how he'd set aside his personal pain to help his cousin with her investigation. She felt at ease with him. Which surprised her. Not exactly an expert at romantic relationships, Tess usually felt as uncomfortable as a junior high girl around attractive single males.

Awkward and studious, she'd been at the receiving end of more than her fair share of geek jokes while growing up. The same thing happened in college. Her brief entry into the collegiate dating scene had ended in disaster. The engineering student she'd considered the love of her life hadn't seen her in the same light. It didn't take her long to realize they had Calculus 101 in common and not much else. After college she kept herself too busy with her career, first as a buyer, then as a department manager, to pay much attention to eligible men.

She shook her head. Enough of that kind of rehashing. A lot of years and growing up had happened since then, and she had a visitor to think of, one who was staring at her, his eyes full of questions.

"Hey!" Ethan's friend Joe called out. "Are you being a lazybones today?"

Ethan shook his head, ran a hand through his dark hair. "No, just saying hi to Tess. But I guess I'm keeping her from her work."

"It's okay," she said. "I needed a break. I've been at this for a while now."

Ethan gave her a smile, one that seemed too bright. "You mean selling junk online."

"Isn't it great?" she asked with equally determined cheer. "I love it. I get to collect all kinds of neat, weird things, and people will actually pay to take them off my hands again. How cool is that?"

He arched a brow. "I'm not ready to call it great or cool, but the weird part I won't argue. What does that say about the entrepreneur?"

"No, no! You're not supposed to ask. I don't want to know." Then she turned to Joe. "Did you need something? Or am I just keeping Ethan from work?"

Joe raised his glass of water. "Thirsty. It's hot today."

"How's the ramp going?" she asked.

"Great!" the two men said, then launched into a discussion of angles and pitch and load that left Tess in the dark.

She leaned back in the chair and watched the friendly back-and-forth. Ethan had insisted on building a ramp from the front walk to the porch for Uncle Gordon. And he'd told her Joe supplemented what he earned in his job at Loganton's Department of Sanitation with the occasional odd job. Installing a basement window and building the ramp were the perfect thing, according to Ethan. And Joe could use the money. He sent his large family back in Mexico every penny he could. As proud as Ethan's friend was of his legal-alien status and his green card, Ethan had described Joe's sadness every time he spoke of his younger siblings and their lack of opportunity.

Tess agreed. It was better to hire Joe than a stranger to do the job. Ethan, as she'd expected, had refused payment for his help.

Just then her laptop chimed. Tess gave it a glance. "Hey! Come take a look. It's my first honest-to-goodness sale!"

Ethan approached her desk. "A mogul is born!"

With a hand on her chair's backrest and the other close to her on the desk, he leaned over her to see. Tess grew flustered. She felt his breath ruffle her hair, saw the ropey muscles on his arm and sensed his warmth surround her. Her pulse kicked up its beat, and she drew in a hitching breath.

Oh, my!

"Well?" he asked. "Are you rich?"

"Um…it sold well," she answered, her heart beating faster still, only too aware of his nearness. "But not *that* well. It…uh…was the urn Miss Tabitha thought would sell for the least amount, and it went for four hundred dollars. Not bad!"

"Urn?" Joe asked stepping inside the sunroom. "What is an urn?"

Ethan straightened, laughing. "Take it away, Miss Mogul!"

"Lucky me!" How did one describe a funerary urn? "It's a jar," she said. "Like a vase but with a foot—a stand. And they have lids on top. People in the 1800s used them to store the ashes of their dead relatives."

The look on Joe's face was priceless. "Dead people?"

"Yeah," she said, laughing. "Go figure."

Joe scratched his chin. "You sold one?"

"Yes, that's what I do." She pointed to her laptop. "That's the kind of work I do."

"Work?" Joe asked.

Tess and Ethan traded looks—and smiles, hers sheepish, his roguish. "I sell things online." She waved at the laptop. "I list the items my clients don't want, and I sell them, using the computer, to people who do want them. I keep a percentage of the money the buyer pays."

"Who bought this urn?" he asked.

Tess shrugged. "I don't really know." She turned to the laptop. "Some woman named Rose...Rose Red is what she calls herself online."

Confusion darkened Joe's eyes. "You don't know this Rose? But she bought an urn from you. How do you know she'll pay?"

Tess grinned. "Ahh...the wonders of the Internet!" She clicked on a couple of icons to find the buyer's profile and payment performance stats. "I know, I know. It sounds crazy. But see? It says here she grows roses in a greenhouse, other sellers say she pays all the time, and she says she's from New York."

"You sold an urn in Loganton to a woman in New York. On the computer?"

Tess nodded.

Ethan chortled.

Joe stared at the monitor. "You have a store? *There?*"

Tess fought back a laugh. "Sort of. An online store."

"Crazy," Joe said. "Some crazy New York woman wanted Miss Tabitha's dead-people jar. On the computer."

"That about sums it up," Tess said, the laughter spilling out.

"*Bah!* It's all crazy." Joe gave the computer another baleful glare, turned and headed for the front door. "I have to finish outside. Goodbye."

As he left, Tess heard him mutter something about dead and crazy people.

Ethan winked. "See what the unsuspecting public thinks of your nutty business?"

"It's a perfectly legitimate business. Lots of people make very good money online. It's not my problem if other people aren't aware of the full potential of the Internet."

His eyebrows came together. "You're right, in more ways than one. Every other day you hear of a new scam. You might want to be extra careful. You don't want to get burned."

"You have a point, but there's risk everywhere. You can't get away from evil. You'd almost have to eliminate a large part of humankind to get rid of greed and crime. That's not the way God works. His plan is for even the worst of criminals to someday come to Him."

A muscle in Ethan's cheek tightened. "I know all that, but I also know what's out there. I can't see drug dealers and cold-blooded killers converting just like that."

Tess stood. "It won't happen just like that, but I can't give up hope." From the look on his face, it seemed Ethan had…or was close to giving up. "That's what faith's all about. And I know God can change lives when we choose to trust Him."

"You sound like Art Reams."

"I've heard more than a few of his sermons."

Ethan shrugged. "Speaking of the good pastor, I'm meeting him later to go over the summer sports programs we're planning for the kids. I'd better go help Joe again. Good luck with your sales."

Tess waved and turned back to her desk. She couldn't deny her attraction to Ethan. Just as she couldn't deny his obvious pain. Whatever had driven him from his former career must have been big. She wondered if he would ever be able to tell her, if he would ever break through the wall of pain she sensed he'd built. She still felt the urge to help him, to ease his pain, to bring back the smile she liked so much.

And then she realized what she'd been doing. "Tess, Tess, Tess! You can't let an attractive man drag your thoughts miles away. Remember your track record—"

The phone rang, cutting her off. "Hello?"

"I warned you." The harsh voice of the other night sent ice through her veins. "I want it back."

Tess clenched her fist on her desk, crumpling a sheet of paper. "Who are you? What do you want?"

"You know—"

"I don't!" Her heart thumped, her ears buzzed, and fear nearly closed her throat. "Tell me who—what…"

"You'll be sorry. Give it back."

The sudden silence set off a series of tremors. She dropped the phone. The room began to spin. Her heart continued its fierce beating, and her breath came out in small gasps.

"Why?" she whispered. "Why is this happening, Lord?"

Tess hoped she wouldn't have to see Maggie Lowe again anytime soon. She had nothing against the police officer, who seemed efficient and thorough, but Tess's nerves were shot after the call.

Even she couldn't try to tell herself they were dealing with a string of strange coincidences. Too much had happened for that even to be a possibility. Someone had threatened her. More than once.

But why? She hadn't been back in Loganton long enough to make anyone angry. And she'd been gone long enough that anyone who'd been angry with her in the past should have gotten on with their life.

No matter how many times Maggie asked, Tess couldn't come up with a reason for the threats. Once the officer left, Tess spent the rest of the afternoon upstairs with her newly barbered dog. While he did look better with his clean fur and clipped claws, he would never win Best in Show. His coat was the color of dirt—even though the real stuff had been washed out—and sparse in spots. Tess hoped the fur would fill in as the little guy grew accustomed to the ultrapremium kibble she'd bought.

But none of that mattered. If she were totally honest, her new pet was still contraband. Ever since she'd brought him home the day before, she'd kept him in her room, playing the radio louder than usual. She hoped the music would muffle any stray yips, barks or whines. This evening could be her undoing.

She'd made plans to attend a new Bible study at church, and since she couldn't take the dog with her or leave him in the car, he had to stay in her room. When she'd asked, Uncle Gordon had said he planned to watch *Wheel of Fortune, Jeopardy* and the news until she was back and could help him up the stairs. She hoped the dog behaved.

After her shower Tess picked out a green knit top and filmy matching skirt. She dried her hair, pulled it back with a wide hair band, and slipped on sandals to accommodate her bandaged foot. Finally she tucked the tiny dog into his carrier and zipped him in. "There you go."

The little guy didn't object, but stared at her through the mesh window. "You know," she murmured as she went to gather her things, "I'm going to have to come up with a good name for you."

With a backward glance, she watched her little friend tilt his head, rub his delicate muzzle against the mesh and stare at her with alert and shiny eyes.

Patty, the groomer, had said he was healthy but urged her to have him checked out by the vet. It looked as though the overdose victim had cared enough about her pet to feed him and see to his most basic needs.

Drawing the door behind her, Tess gave him one last look. "You be good now."

Partway down the stairs, she noticed a delicious aroma, she took a detour via the kitchen, where she walked in on a major cooking extravaganza. "Whoa!" Tess exclaimed. "What are you guys doing?"

Uncle Gordon and Miss Tabitha sat on either side of the large farm table, each peeling a mountain of shrimp. Piles of chopped veggies lined one end, while a sack of rice, jars of home-canned tomatoes, herbs, spices and a whole lot more covered the counters from end to end. The smell of sautéed…something filled the air with mouthwatering fragrance.

"We're testing recipes," Miss Tabitha said.

Uncle Gordon grinned. "Want to try our jambalaya?"

"Just a taste. Remember? I'm going to that new Bible study at church."

"Oh, yeah." Her uncle scooped up a pile of savory rice and other good things and handed her the large cooking spoon. "I did forget."

"Yum!" Tess munched happily, then dropped the spoon in the sink. "Is there a reason for this—" she waved "—excess?"

The two seniors traded a conspiratorial look. Tess leaned against the counter and braced herself. Life with Uncle Gordon was never boring.

"Come on, you two," she teased. "Let me in on the secret. I know you can't eat all that by yourselves. Are you having a party?"

Uncle Gordon turned to Miss Tabitha. "Go ahead. You tell her. You'll do better'n me."

Miss Tabitha gave Tess a smile. "Seeing as you're the one who gave me the idea in the first place, Tess, I think you're going to love our plans."

"Me?" *Oh, boy.* "What bright idea did I give you?"

"We've decided to follow in your footsteps," Miss Tabitha said. "We're going into business. The cooking school business."

Okay. She had given Miss Tabitha the idea. "Here?"

"Of course," Uncle Gordon said. "Tabby's got all them boarders at her place. You can't just go bringing in more people at all hours to teach 'em how to cook. Nothing happens here, so this is the perfect place."

"Besides," Miss Tabitha added. "This kitchen's bigger than mine. And this table is perfect for food prep. We'll set up chairs down one end, and our students can watch us make the dishes right in front of them."

"Have you figured out costs? Taxes? Health Department licenses?"

Her uncle pointed at a pile of official-looking papers. "Yep, yep and yep."

"You guys had to have been thinking about this before I said anything to Miss Tabitha. You can't get all that worked out in a couple of days."

Uncle Gordon plopped a handful of raw shrimp into the bowl in front of him. "I'd been trying to talk Tabby into it for a long time. You gave her the final nudge." He sent Tess his most impish grin. "Thanks!"

Tess's head spun. A cooking school in her own home. Who would have thought? Then again, Uncle Gordon had never taken to the idea of retirement. "Okay. Then how about class plans? How many dishes do you plan to make for each session?"

"Oh, maybe three or four." Uncle Gordon shrugged as he stood. He took a moment to balance himself on the walker and then clumped over to the stove. "Tabby's boarders eat up a storm every day. Can't see 'em turning down anything we make. Maybe that Ethan boy can stop by and pick up the food."

From the stove he made his way to the sink. Tess took notice of his progress with the walker. He was getting better at it. But she wasn't going to let him dodge her question. "Are you going to tell me when classes start?"

At the sink, he pumped a squirt of detergent, sudsed his hands and rinsed. Towel in hand, he faced Tess again. "Tabby and I put notices in the grocery store, at the library, in the post office and a little ad in the paper. First one's tomorrow."

Hmm…why did she suddenly have a sinking feeling? It was too late to make them reconsider, so she hoped the classes didn't end in disaster. "I hope you know what you're doing." She waved. "I'll be back in about two hours. See ya!"

Tess got behind the wheel of her uncle's land-yacht, and drove the few blocks to church. She would rather have walked, but everyone, including Ethan and Maggie Lowe, had insisted she drive anytime she needed to go out. They'd said her foot couldn't take much walking.

She knew they weren't worried about her foot. It was the intruder and the caller, that worried them.

Tess hated having to live her life based on what a criminal might or might not do. As she pulled into the church parking lot, she came to a decision. Yes, something strange was going on. But she wasn't going to let it dominate her life. She'd have to watch herself.

She also had to know why someone wanted to terrorize her, what he wanted, what he thought she might have. And she wasn't going to sit around waiting for the police to tie it all up with a neat bow…in their own sweet time.

Not when she had a former DEA agent hanging around the house.

She was going to pray some more about it, but she was fairly sure what her next move would be. Tomorrow morning, bright and early, she would call Ethan and ask for his help.

* * *

As Tess reached the door of the church, someone called her name.

She turned and smiled at Ethan. "Hey! I didn't know you'd be here. Bible study?"

He nodded. "Art's teaching on King David. You know, 'the good, the bad and the ugly'. How about you?"

"Mine's on 'the fruit of the Spirit.' Allison Reams is a great teacher."

"The two of them make a great *team*. This church is lucky to have them." He opened the door, and Tess stepped out into the beautiful spring night. He took her elbow to escort her to the sidewalk.

"Thanks," she said, "again. It seems that's all I do these days. Thank you, that is. You've done so much for us."

He winked. "What? Walking a beautiful, injured woman down a set of stairs? Man, if all hardships were only like that!"

A ripple of pleasure ran through Tess. Did he really think she was beautiful or had he just said it as a throw-away line? Another glance, and she realized his gaze hadn't budged. His smile was genuine and warm.

Wow! Maybe this time she'd do better at this man-woman relationship thing.

"You did drive, didn't you?" he asked.

"Are you kidding? I doubt Uncle Gordon and Miss Tabitha would have let me out the door otherwise."

"Good. I'll go with you to the car."

They fell silent, and Tess grew antsy. "Did they tell you what they're up to?"

"Who? Miss Tabitha and Mr. Graver?"

"Yeah. They're opening a cooking school. In our kitchen."

"Lucky you! Imagine all that good food."

She grimaced. "It's going to go straight to my hips."

"What hips? You look great!"

Tess met his gaze and couldn't look away. Was it more than just polite friendship she found there? She hoped she wasn't seeing what she wanted to find instead of what was really there.

As the moment lengthened, by the light of the nearby streetlight she again noted the deep blue of Ethan's eyes. And then she realized he was staring at her as intensely as she studied him. She felt his gaze trace her features, her forehead, her cheeks, her lips. Her thoughts went into a heady spin.

In the lengthening silence, Ethan reached out and tucked her hair behind her ear. "I've wanted to do that since I first saw—"

Brakes squealed.

An engine roared.

"Run!" Ethan yelled as he pushed Tess sideways and took off himself.

A black van flew over the curb, hit the brakes again, backed up and made for Tess.

She started toward the car but froze when the headlights' beam hit her. She couldn't breathe, couldn't think. She could only feel more fear than she'd ever known before.

"Tess!" Ethan called again. "Get in the church! *Move!*"

Tess heard a car door slam and the van's engine approached. Her feet refused to obey. She tried to take a step, faltered, stopped. The pain from her injury penetrated the haze, and she gasped. The van sped closer by the second. She spun and lunged away from the oncoming bumper.

Her foot took the brunt of her weight. Pain seared her foot and up her leg. Tess cried out, then her leg gave way. As she fell, something snagged the back of her skirt. She heard it rip.

She hit the blacktop with a thump, first her hip then her shoulder. Finally her head hit the pavement. Pain shot through her, especially from her forehead. She tried to blink, but her eyelids felt like lead weights, and she struggled to string together a thought. She had to get up, run, but she could barely breathe. *Lord...help!*

Then she heard another car come close. That vehicle went past her.

From somewhere off to her left, Tess heard the driver of the van gun his engine again. She was fast out of options. She couldn't stand, couldn't put a plan together. She only knew pain. Determined not to give up, she gathered her strength and opened her eyes. It hurt, but she persevered and focused on the cross on the church's steeple, prepared to roll away a second before the tires struck. She prayed again, trying to trust and not fear.

The hideous screech of metal against metal told her the two vehicles had collided. Then...nothing.

Nothing but the screech of tires against pavement, an engine at full throttle pulling away, and then...silence.

A car door slammed shut. Footsteps pounded the pavement. "Tess!" Ethan called. "Are you okay?"

Tess dragged herself up to her feet. She tried to answer, but her chest hurt and her throat burned. She must have been screaming during the whole ordeal, but she had no conscious memory of saying anything. All she knew was the horror she'd felt, the reality of being hunted.

She turned toward Ethan...swayed. Darkness deepened, and the world started to whirl. When Ethan reached her side, Tess fell into his embrace.

SIX

Tess slumped against Ethan's chest. The momentary relief he'd felt when she stood vanished. "Tess!"

She didn't respond—not good.

From the boneless way she lay in his arms, Ethan knew she'd lost consciousness. She needed help, and his hands were full holding her. Bile rose in his throat as bad memories from a year ago came back.

In spite of all his efforts, all the time he'd worked to track Moreno, all the field agents who'd collaborated on the bust, they'd failed—*he'd* failed. He'd been the lead in the operation, and Robby Stoddard had died. Steve now lived in a wheelchair, the field job he'd loved so much only a memory. And Moreno had gotten away.

He tightened his arms around Tess. He'd failed yet again. The maniac in the van hadn't lost control. He'd aimed, sped and then, when he'd missed, backed up and tried again. Ethan had tried to deflect the van away from Tess with his SUV, but had only hit the bumper as the van backed away toward the street. Tess lay unconscious in his arms because he'd failed to keep her safe.

He couldn't bear for her to die.

He'd do anything to see her through this.

Then? He'd have time to think then.

"Ethan!"

A shudder shook him hard.

"You have to let her go."

He blinked. Kaleidoscopic figures swam before his eyes and eventually turned into his cousin, a second cop, Art Reams and two EMTs. Tess still lay in his arms.

"What…?"

"Let her go," Maggie said. "The guys can't help her if you keep holding on."

He'd lived that same reluctance in the alley after Robby had breathed his last; Ethan hadn't been able to let go. They'd pulled the boy away, stood Ethan up and sent him after the third suspect that night. He'd responded automatically, his years of training carrying him through. He'd trapped Moreno's flunky before the guy could join his boss.

But that was a year ago. Tess? Tess was today.

At his cousin's gentle insistence, he grudgingly eased his hold. Reason told him Maggie was right. And Tess was still breathing, even if in shallow bursts.

Once the EMTs took possession of his precious armful, the pounding in his head slowed beat by slow beat, and he told himself, more than once, he was no longer in a drug-infested alley or on the worst of Chicago's mean streets.

He met Maggie's gaze. "Sorry."

The flashback had hit with the force of a runaway

train. He'd thought he was better; the memories had only haunted him late at night, in his dreams, the last few weeks. But when Tess collapsed against him, his mind transported him in the span of an instant to the night Robby Stoddard died in his arms.

Dear God! Not Tess, please. Don't let her—

He couldn't even voice the hideous possibility in a prayer. He couldn't stand the thought of losing Tess.

Not that she was his to lose.

"Is she—" His voice sounded rough even to his own ears. "Will she be okay?"

One of the emergency technicians glanced up. "She's got a deep cut on her forehead and a concussion, at the very least. A neurologist will probably order a CT scan, and that'll show what's going on. They'll be looking to see if there's bleeding on the brain. I can't tell you how bad it is or how she's going to respond."

Neurologist…head injury.

Ethan's gut churned as the two professionals strapped Tess onto a gurney. He remembered her reaction when the EMTs carried the overdose victim out of the woods. The only difference between the two women's situations was that one lay cold in the morgue, and the other…the other would, if it were in God's will, live.

The men guided the gurney to the ambulance, and Maggie placed a hand on his shoulder. "Can you tell me what happened?"

He ran a hand over his face, then shoved both fists into his pockets. He rolled his stiff shoulders, breathed deep, stretched his neck to the left and the right; nothing eased his tension.

Ethan sighed. "A van tried to mow her down, Mags. It was no accident. When he didn't get her right off, he backed up and tried again. Check the fender of my SUV and the pavement. I'm sure you'll find traces of paint and burnt rubber tracks."

When the EMTs went to shut the ambulance's back doors, Ethan called out. "Hey! Wait up. I'm going with her."

The two men turned to Maggie, who shook her head. "We have to follow you guys to the hospital. I'll get him there."

Ethan was about to argue, but he remembered that his little cousin, not so little anymore, was the officer in charge. He was only a witness, a civilian these days. Nothing, however, could change the way he felt. He had to be with Tess.

He walked ahead of the officers to the cruiser. Its white paint glowed in the dark, a beacon of order in a disordered world. His need to do something fueled his pace. "Let's go, then," he called over his shoulder.

Before he could get into the car, Maggie's partner, a stocky older man with a blond buzz haircut, reached the driver's side door. He crossed his arms and shot questioning looks, first at Ethan and then at Mags.

"Wayne Donelly," his cousin said with an ironic twist to her voice, "meet my cousin Ethan, formerly with the DEA."

Understanding spread over the blunt features. "I

figured sooner or later I'd get a chance to meet you." The officer held out his hand and Ethan shook it. "Sorry it's like this."

The three climbed into the car, Wayne behind the wheel, Ethan in the rear seat. Safety belts clicked, and then Maggie, in the front passenger seat, turned at an awkward angle to meet Ethan's gaze. "How about you give me an idea what went down back there?"

Ethan tamped down the wave of nausea to give his best recounting of the attempt on Tess's life. Finally, when he'd described everything he could remember, he said the only thing left to say. "Why? Why would anyone want to hurt Tess?"

"I'd say," his cousin answered, her expression grim, "it's my job to find out."

"You don't have to ask," he said. "I'll help any way I can."

"I figured as much."

Ethan shot Maggie a questioning look. He'd never heard her words so clipped, her voice so tight. She didn't answer; she only shook her head.

At the hospital Ethan learned he'd have to wait until Tess was moved to a regular room before he could see her again. Since she was still unconscious and a neurologist was on his way to examine her, that move wouldn't happen anytime soon. The wait promised to be excruciating. And he didn't want to examine why he felt the way he did.

"Someone's going to have to tell her uncle," he said. "Do you want me to do it?"

Maggie shook her head. "It's my job, Ethan. I can handle it just fine."

"But someone's going to have to bring him here. And if you plan to do it, you'll need help. Let me go with you. You know nothing's going to keep Gordon Graver from his niece the minute he knows she's been hurt."

Wayne gave Ethan a friendly slap on the back. "I'll help Maggie here with Gordon. You stay with your girl. She's going to be mighty glad to see you when she wakes up."

"Tess isn't 'my girl.'" Ethan frowned. What *was* Tess to him? "We've just met. At most, we're new friends."

Wayne's brown eyes took a quick trip over Ethan's tight shoulders and fisted hands. "Okay, son. If you say so."

Maggie clamped her lips tighter but wouldn't meet Ethan's gaze.

He shrugged and waved his hands in defeat. "Fine. Go ahead and get Gordon. Just go easy telling him about Tess. He's no spring chicken, you know."

Wayne hooted as he walked toward the rotating door. "Don't give it a thought. Gordon Graver's got more vinegar in his veins than most men half his age. He'll be fine. You'll see."

Before Ethan could say anything else, Maggie came straight over to his side. "I'll be right behind you," she called after her partner then turned to Ethan. She swallowed hard and pulled herself to her full height, her expression somber. She then met his gaze head-on. "Ethan, there's something you should know. We got back the autopsy results on the overdose victim this afternoon."

Icy fingers of dread licked up the back of Ethan's neck. "And...?"

She cleared her throat before going on. "And there's more there than we first thought. At the time I was pretty sure I could see signs of a struggle, and my guys were able to document it. The victim had the bruising to go along with a fight."

Ethan clenched his jaw. "It happens all the time when drugs are involved."

Maggie glanced at the double doors to the E.R. "It's more than that."

She let out a harsh breath. "Okay. Sarah McVee died of a methamphetamine overdose, just as I thought. The autopsy determined she habitually smoked the stuff." When Maggie finally met his gaze, the chill of fear balled in his stomach. She went on. "But the medical examiner found one—only one—needle track on her arm. That's the dose that killed her, not the meth she smoked. And..."

Maggie paused, looked away. "She also had blunt trauma to the head. The coroner feels the guy who pushed Tess into the mud probably knocked our victim out. He believes the injection came after the blow to the head."

Ethan ran a hand through his hair. A struggle...an unconscious woman...an injection site. Most recreational meth users didn't inject. "Murder," he said.

But it was Maggie's next statement that made his heart really sink. "Ethan. There's more. The only prints at the scene came from the victim and Tess."

* * *

From where she lay, in the depths of the pit, Tess made out a series of sounds. A voice…a beep…a thump. She reached toward the sounds, but the darkness bound her.

No, no more.

She fought to open her eyes and the haze lightened momentarily. Then darkness shrouded her again.

After a nurse stopped by to tell him Tess would soon return from the CT scan but hadn't yet regained consciousness, Ethan prowled the hospital halls to find the waiting room. There he spent what felt like hours but amounted to little more than thirty minutes' worth of back-and-forth pacing. He tried to watch the TV hung high on the wall, but the cable news channel failed to keep his attention. The tang of antiseptic products stung his nose, and the hushed, anxious whispers of other patients' family members kept his nerves on edge.

Could he have misjudged Tess? She'd seemed innocent, showed no obvious signs of drug abuse, yet she'd been at the scene of the crime, reported it. Hers were the only prints there besides those of the victim, the murdered victim. What did that mean?

Could she be a drug dealer? Not all drug dealers partook of the wares they peddled, so she didn't need to be a user to be involved. Most only cared about the money they could extort from the poor souls into whom they sank their hooks.

Ethan ran a hand through his hair, irritated by his

misstep. He didn't know what to believe. He hadn't been gone from the agency that long. He should have been more on his game. The longer he stewed, the angrier he grew. He was angry at the situation and, most of all, at himself for dropping his guard.

He had to build it back up.

He had to be far more vigilant with his errant feelings. He couldn't let himself be drawn into a relationship with Tess. He had to help Maggie solve a crime. Should Tess be involved—and he hoped, really hoped, she wasn't— and if there was any way to stop her, he would find it. Tess couldn't be left to harm anyone again…

If, if she was involved. The possibility of innocence remained, no matter how bad things looked, until evidence proved it beyond a shadow of a doubt. Besides, someone was clearly out to get her. Maybe she was just an innocent victim.

Ethan would have to find the patience to wait. Her recovery could take days, maybe even weeks. He had to wait until she was strong enough to answer his questions, well enough that she wouldn't think she could use her injuries and pain as a shield.

What would Tess do if she learned of his suspicions?

He had to watch her every move. That was the only way he could prove her innocence. He had to back up and become neutral.

That gave him another good reason to build, if nothing else, emotional distance, a wall of reserve, between them. A cool, sober front was what he needed to present. Until he knew.

"Ethan, son!" He turned to see a pale and distraught Gordon Graver wield his walker around an armchair, a side table, and across an aisle to his side. "How's my girl? The cops told me she hit her head bad."

Miss Tabitha followed, her cheeks wet with tears, her eyes red, lips tight and white. "I'm so thankful you were with her."

"She was still unconscious when the ambulance brought her in," he said. "Since I'm not a family member, they wouldn't let me go with her, and no one's come out to tell me anything yet. I only know a neurologist ordered a CT scan to check how her brain is doing."

The senior citizens exchanged troubled looks.

"Is there anyone we could talk to?" Mr. Graver asked. "Should we go look?"

Miss Tabitha, arms hugged tight around her chest, turned to Ethan for a response.

What an impossible situation to find himself in. "The staff knows I'm waiting," Ethan said. "I'm sure someone will come as soon as they can."

He stepped forward to take the walker when Miss Tabitha went to help Mr. Graver to the nearest armchair. She took the adjoining seat, reached for a knobby-fingered hand and then faced Ethan. "You look all done in. Why don't you join us?"

He doubted a caged tiger in any zoo could feel more frustrated than he. He wanted answers, and he wanted them *now*. But Ethan knew that was unreasonable, so he called again on his will and pushed back the urge to learn the truth right away. What he needed was an extra measure of patience, a virtue he sometimes lacked. He sat at Mr. Graver's right.

"Well," Miss Tabitha said after a bit. "We're doing Tess no good fretting like this. Let's pray."

Ethan refused to sit in judgment without more evidence than Maggie had so far, no matter how bad it looked. Tess could very well have arrived at the scene as she'd said, only to escape meeting the same fate as Sarah McVee by nothing more than the grace of a merciful God.

As soon as she regained consciousness, and he knew she would recover, he'd start to look into who Tess Graver really was. He would dig deep, learn everything there was to know about her. He would uncover her innocence or guilt. God expected as much from him.

He took Miss Tabitha's hand and they prayed.

As the sun's glow crept over the horizon, Ethan finally persuaded Mr. Graver and Miss Tabitha to go home. They'd been allowed to see Tess in the head-trauma center, and Mr. Graver had made sure everyone in the hospital, from the nurses at the charge desk to the president in his bed at home, knew Ethan could stay with Tess as long as he liked. But her condition remained unchanged.

"Tess would want you to take care of yourselves. I'll let you know the minute she comes to," he said for the fourth time. "I promise."

Miss Tabitha agreed before Mr. Graver finally surrendered. In the end, it took the additional weight of Art Reams's persuasive powers to pry the older man from his niece's side.

After they left, Ethan crossed the room to Tess's bed and gripped the cold side rail. He studied her pretty face, unfamiliar in its ethereal stillness. She was pale, her normally animated features resembling carved wax. As he followed their lines with his gaze, he felt the knot of his anger ease. Even unconscious, she tugged at his emotions in a way no else did.

Seeing her like this, leashed by tubes to a wide assortment of beeping and blinking machines, disturbed him. Every sound, every light, heightened his anxiety. He wished he could will her awake. "Tess?"

He watched and waited for a response, a blink or a twitch—anything—but nothing moved. Only the steady in-and-out of her breath assured him she was still alive. Before he could stop himself, Ethan reached out a finger and ran it down her cheek. Warm and silky, her skin inspired him to explore some more. He outlined her brow, her cheekbone, her jaw all the way down to her chin; he stopped just under her lips.

He missed Tess's bright smile.

Aside from holding her upright a time or two, he'd only touched Tess when he'd tucked her hair behind her ear seconds before the van came flying over the curb. Now, with a cloud of suspicion hanging over her, he really shouldn't be touching her at all.

Hands back in his pockets, Ethan walked to the window to watch the sun chase the night's darkness away. He wished the morning could as easily wipe the worst memories and new suspicions from his mind.

A nurse walked in to check on Tess, something that

happened round the clock. Once the young woman was done, Ethan sat in the vinyl chair by the bed, elbows on his knees. He hated feeling useless, but at the moment there was nothing he could do. Tess was in God's hands.

At the break of the new day, Ethan faced a stark and simple truth. He wanted Tess to get well, not just for her sake, but also for the chance to prove the evidence wrong. He wanted Tess to come out on the other side victorious, cleared and innocent. He wanted his feelings for her to have the chance to grow.

He also hoped she sensed God's presence. He hoped the doctors and nurses would have the wisdom and skill to care for her. As for himself, he needed to uncover the truth. What had really happened out in the woods?

In the fresh, clear morning light, Ethan faced his greatest fear. If Tess was guilty, he would need God's strength to deal with the truth. He would also need God's comfort, and not just for himself. He would have to comfort Mr. Graver and Miss Tabitha through their grief as well.

Tess floated through the darkness. A momentary flash of light, a spark of hope, pierced the void. She tried to reach it, but her arms refused to do her bidding, weighted down as they felt. A vise tightened around her head, and the murkiness closed over her again.

Fear numbed her, fear so great it stole her ability to think, to reason. She sank back into the pit of pain.

Without any sense of time, she floated again. A familiar voice called her name, over and over and over again, from somewhere beyond the dark. Another flicker of hope pierced the shadows with its fingers of light. She fought against the bonds holding her in the dark, reaching deep for what strength she could summon.

Up…up…up…then her eyes opened. The brilliant glow blinded her, and she closed her eyes again. But after her time in the dark, she wanted to cling to the light. On the other side, out in the brilliance, something beeped.

Again that familiar voice called her name. She parted her lips to answer, but nothing happened. As the darkness threatened to swallow her again, she moved her eyes, fluttered her lids, saw more light, and then faces took form.

"Tessie!" Uncle Gordon cried, joy in his voice.

"Oh, my dear…" Miss Tabitha said on a sob.

Tess felt the smile start in her heart. It spread warmth through her cold limbs and then curved her lips. "Hi," she said in little more than a whisper.

A third face came into focus not more than five feet away. Ethan!

Bits of memory drifted back. Tess remembered the tender moment when he'd smoothed her hair, how he'd looked in the golden glow of the streetlight, the hideous shriek of screeching brakes…a black van only inches away. She remembered fear, gut-wrenching fear for her life. She also remembered Ethan's deep voice telling her to run, as his hands pushed her out of the way, his body shielding her as the van approached.

She remembered pain unlike anything she'd ever known. Through that haze, she remembered he'd run to her aid, even after the van had carried on its onslaught. She remembered the sweet relief when he reached her side.

"Thank…you…for…saving…my life."

SEVEN

"Tess?" Her name floated to her from some distance away. "Can you wake up?" he asked. "You did it before."

She willed her eyelids to open and saw deep blue eyes staring down at her. He repeated her name and took hold of her hand. His touch sent wonderful warmth up her arm as she recognized her companion.

"Ethan? What…?"

"You hit your head when you fell. Do you remember?"

Tess grasped at wisps of thought, but they eluded her efforts. She blinked, and the minute motion shot pain through her head. "Hurts…"

She let her eyes drift closed. Darkness beckoned. Sleep would bring relief. But before oblivion enfolded her, another voice, this one female, joined his. "Miss Graver?"

"Tess…"

"Please wake up."

When she made her eyes obey again, she was rewarded with a blast of searing white light.

* * *

The next time Tess waded up from the dark, she managed to hold her eyes open and tolerate the light. This time, Uncle Gordon stood at her side, his veiny hands tight on a metal rail. "Praise God, she's awake!" he called.

Tess blinked and it didn't hurt as much as it had before. Miss Tabitha's sweet face joined her uncle's in her line of sight.

Tess's mouth felt full of cotton. "Thirsty…"

"Here," Ethan said from her other side.

Her eyes flew open. The movement detonated a fresh quake of pain inside her head. But as she moaned, something prodded her lips. Willing it so, she clamped her mouth around the straw and drew in a drip of liquid coolness.

"Careful," he added, pulling the straw away.

"More!"

He nodded. "There you go, Mr. Graver. She's getting better."

The straw returned to her mouth, and Tess drank again. When it became too much effort to sip, she pushed against the straw with her tongue. Ethan took it away.

She blinked again and felt as though some of the gauze inside her thoughts was wiped away, so she blinked again and again. When she made herself focus, her gaze landed on a TV up high. Strange.

Where was she? A metal rail…wall hung TV…the straw. "I'm in the hospital?" she whispered.

"Don't you remember?" Ethan asked, a scowl on his face. "You must remember the van."

Tess sucked in a harsh breath. Her heart sped to a heavy pounding and her instinct was to run again, to flee, to live. Darkness encroached on the edge of her vision. She fought against its hungry grasp. Her gaze flew from Uncle Gordon to Ethan to Miss Tabitha and the TV, her hand reaching for something to anchor her, something to keep her on this side of the light.

"It's okay, Tessie," her uncle said, taking her right hand in his. "You're safe. Nothing's going to hurt you here."

"I shouldn't have asked," Ethan asked, his cool fingers against hers. "The doctors have said you'll have trouble remembering. They think you'll get your memory back soon, when the swelling in your brain is gone."

"Swelling in my brain…" *Brain damage?* "Ooooh…"

The last thing she heard was Ethan's deep voice calling to her.

A handful of hours after she woke up for real a pair of orderlies rolled Tess from the head trauma unit to a regular room. Fortunately her brain had suffered only a small contusion, a bruise. The neurologist who stopped by to check on her progress once they'd settled her in confirmed what Ethan and Miss Tabitha had said. She didn't like it but had to accept his prognosis. He said she'd have memory blanks for a while to come, and the frequent spells of confusion could take even longer to clear.

Tess had no reason to complain. She knew she was lucky to be alive. The driver of the van had meant to kill her. That much was etched in her memory; no bump to the head would dislodge it.

But she did chafe at the frequent disruptions. It seemed as though a nurse, neurology intern or member of the army of lab techs intent on bleeding her dry— waited until she fell asleep to then pounce.

Her body had become little more than a sack of aches and pains, and she was only allowed mild acetamino-phen for the pain. They insisted on keeping her mind as clear as possible at all times so they could continue to evaluate the condition of her brain.

Tess sighed. She couldn't wait until they let her go back home again. TV didn't satisfy for long. She now knew how her uncle had felt. She wanted out.

As she thought she'd lose her mind to the boredom, Ethan walked in. His features wore the same serious ex-pression she'd come to expect since she'd regained con-sciousness. "I see your smile's upside down again," she said by way of greeting.

"I suppose the next thing you're going to ask is how soon you can go home."

"Well? Can you tell me?"

"It's been less than twenty-four hours since you hit your head. They're going to keep you at least through tomorrow. If you're lucky, you can bargain your release for the day after."

Tess groaned. "I know I'm lucky. It could have been so much worse, but I *hate* hospitals."

"Pretty strong feelings."

"Look, I've lost my mom, dad and great-aunt. Whenever I walk into one of these places, it's never for a good thing. And then the old sadness and loss hit me again. It's not so hard to understand."

He raised his hands in the universal sign of surrender. "Got it. But you still have to stay put."

Then a stray thought occurred to her. "Don't get me wrong, Ethan. I appreciate everything you've done for me, but…don't you have anything better to do than hang around my hospital room? Don't you work?"

To Tess, who'd thought her question reasonable and logical, it felt as though a brick wall dropped down between them. The lines of Ethan's features tightened. His brow furrowed; his eyes blazed. His shoulders drew back and down, and his hands fisted at his sides.

Wow!

"That wasn't the best way to ask." Tess breathed deep, clamped her lips tight as she gathered her admittedly fuzzy thoughts, before she pressed the up button for the top half of her bed.

Feeling somewhat more in control, she continued. "You have to admit, Ethan, a man of your age doesn't normally hang around to watch a near stranger sleep for days. I've wondered ever since we met what it is you do. How do you support yourself? I never asked because I thought it too impolite to ask, but…"

"Now you don't."

"Not so much." She raised a shoulder. "If I count all the hours you've spent with me here, then we're old pals. I don't have any secrets, and I'd like to know a bit about you. It's only fair."

His brows drew a fraction closer, deepening the lines between them. "Fair. Hmm…"

With obvious effort, he adopted a relaxed stance. "You already know a lot about me. You know I'm a former DEA agent, you know I moved here after I retired, you know I'm Maggie Lowe's older cousin, and you know I love Miss Tabitha and her meals."

"There's more to you than that," she prodded.

"If you really have to know, I invested my earnings from the agency for years. I've always lived a simple life, and still do. Since I left Chicago, I've been living off that. Don't worry. I'm not cheating Miss Tabitha out of her rent." Then, with a shake of his head, he paused as if to tether his emotions again. "It's more than that. I…I've been seeking God's will for the rest of my life."

Tess nodded slowly. "Okay. I can buy that. I didn't mean to set you off. I just wanted to get to know you better."

He struggled. An array of emotions chased over his face. Then, as she thought he might say more, he spun and stalked to the window, hands in his pockets, shoulders stiff, head erect.

Great. So much for progress. Although his body still stood in her hospital room, Ethan the man had gone miles away.

Electric energy filled the room. Tension stretched between them. Then, as she was about to withdraw her request, he spoke, his voice like a rusty wheel.

"Robby Stoddard was seventeen years old," he said.

We'd like to send you two free books to introduce you to the Love Inspired® Suspense series. Your two books have a combined cover price of $11.00 in the U.S. and $13.00 in Canada, but they are yours free! We'll even send you two wonderful surprise gifts. You can't lose!

Each of your **FREE** books is filled with riveting inspirational suspense featuring Christian characters facing challenges to their faith... and their lives!

GET 2 **FREE** BOOKS!

HURRY!
Return this card today to get **2 FREE Books** *and* **2 FREE** *Bonus Gifts!*

Love Inspired. SUSPENSE

YES! *Please send me the 2 FREE Love Inspired® Suspense books and 2 FREE gifts for which I qualify. I understand that I am under no obligation to purchase anything further, as explained on the back of this card.*

affix free books sticker here

323 IDL ERRT   123 IDL ERQ5

FIRST NAME   LAST NAME

ADDRESS

APT.#   CITY

STATE/PROV.   ZIP/POSTAL CODE

Steeple Hill Reader Service — Here's How It Works:

Accepting your 2 free books and 2 free gifts places you under no obligation to buy anything. You may keep the books and gifts and return the shipping statement marked "cancel." If you do not cancel, about a month later we will send you 4 additional books and bill you just $4.24 each in the U.S. or $4.74 each in Canada, plus 25¢ shipping & handling per book and applicable taxes if any.* That's the complete price, and — compared to cover prices of $5.50 each in the U.S. and $6.50 each in Canada — it's quite a bargain! You may cancel at any time, but if you choose to continue, every month we'll send you 4 more books, which you may either purchase at the discount price...or return to us and cancel your subscription.

*Terms and prices subject to change without notice. Sales tax applicable in N.Y. Canadian residents will be charged applicable provincial taxes and GST. All orders subject to approval. Books received may not be as shown. Credit or debit balances in a customer's account(s) may be offset by any other outstanding balance owed by or to the customer. Please allow 4 to 6 weeks for delivery. Offer available while quantities last.

BUSINESS REPLY MAIL
FIRST-CLASS MAIL   PERMIT NO. 717   BUFFALO, NY

POSTAGE WILL BE PAID BY ADDRESSEE

STEEPLE HILL READER SERVICE
3010 WALDEN AVE
PO BOX 1867
BUFFALO NY 14240-9952

NO POSTAGE
NECESSARY
IF MAILED
IN THE
UNITED STATES

If offer card is missing write to: Steeple Hill Reader Service, 3010 Walden Ave., P.O. Box 1867, Buffalo, NY 14240-1867

"He got hooked on meth when he turned fifteen." He took a deep breath, raising and dropping his shoulders. "To support his habit, he turned to dealing the stuff—at school. He was only one of dozens. Ernesto Moreno, Robby's supplier, controls the kids' lives with an iron will."

Tightness in her chest told Tess she'd been holding her breath. She exhaled softly, unwilling to distract him from his tale.

"We spent months gathering evidence," he continued. "We tracked Moreno's trail of ruined lives. We were there that night, ready to nab him before he put any more poison in another kid's hands. But..."

"But something went wrong," she said in a whisper.

He turned, and her heart ached at the emotion in his face. "He'd decided Robby had exhausted his usefulness. He refused to supply the kid with more meth. Robby objected and..."

"You don't have to..." Tess let her words die off; she didn't need to hear any more. She raised a hand to stop him, but his gaze was fixed on events only he could see in his mind.

As if she'd never spoken, Ethan ran a shaky hand through his hair. "Robby died in my arms. Moreno shot him, shot my partner then slipped past all of us and right out of the alley. My partner's in a wheelchair. The surgeons couldn't remove Moreno's bullet—too close to the spine." He paused, sighed. "We got the third guy, one of Moreno's flunkies. His trial's coming up soon. I have to testify."

Inadequate though they were, the words slipped between her lips. "I'm sorry."

When she could no longer bear to see the ravages of his emotions, Tess closed her eyes. In her mind, a strong man's arms held a dying boy close. Tears welled up. Ethan had every right to take time to heal.

Then, in a sudden memory of her attack, she saw Ethan running toward her in the dark. Pain gripped her head, and the fear came back, making it hard to breathe. Then sudden understanding came to Tess. She finally got it. The reason for his frowns; it was pain, not anger, she saw.

Ethan must have felt as though history had repeated itself when she'd fallen into his arms. At that moment Ethan had probably relived the helplessness he'd felt that other night in a Chicago back alley.

And his constant presence at her side? Tess felt certain she understood that, too. Because he hadn't been able to do anything for Robby, Ethan had done everything in his power for her, even if the only things he'd had to offer were his company and his prayers.

In the two days after Ethan gave Tess a glimpse of his pain, she didn't see him. Then he called, insisting on driving Tess home from the hospital. She accepted his offer.

Once in the SUV, she turned. "Why?"

He turned the key in the ignition. "Why what?"

"Why did you want to take me home? First you spent hours by my side in the hospital, and then you disappeared for two days. Now you won't let anyone else take me home. I don't get it."

He slanted her a look with a hint of humor. "You'll see."

Talk about feeling disoriented! Tess doubted this was what the neurologists had in mind when they alerted her to possible spells of confusion in the days to come. She lowered her gaze to her lap and pinched the bridge of her nose with her index finger and thumb.

"Um…" he started, after a bit. "I…uh…I'm sorry about the other day. It wasn't the time or place. I shouldn't have unloaded on you."

"Hey! I pushed." Tess reached out and put a hand on his shoulder, careful not to startle him or distract him from the traffic on the road. "I shouldn't have pried, but I do appreciate your trust. You have nothing to apologize for. I can't begin to imagine going through something like that."

He gave a brief nod. "Thanks. And I'm glad you're well enough to go home."

The awkwardness between them was so thick she would have needed a surgeon's scalpel to cut through it. A quick look out the window, and she sighed in relief. They were almost home.

As he pulled up in front of the big yellow house, Tess noticed a number of vehicles parked along the street. She started to ask, but Ethan opened his door.

"Wait for me," he said as he got out.

He opened her door and slipped an arm around her waist. Tess faltered, and not from her injuries. The woodsy scent of his cologne or maybe aftershave tickled her nose, and Tess leaned closer. She liked his looks, his scent, his strength, even the depth of his feelings. She wished he weren't so deeply scarred by the horrors he'd seen. She suspected Robby had only been the last of many blows. Maybe she could—

Oh, no. No you don't.

As they walked up the porch ramp, Tess reminded herself she had no experience with men. She had no business with wishes or maybes, not if they had anything to do with Ethan Rogers and the demons from his past.

"Surprise, surprise," he murmured, throwing open the front door.

She shot him a look. The slight curve of his lips reminded her of his earlier, easy grins, and she found herself responding with a smile, against her better judgment. Then she heard what had to be the "surprise."

A gaggle of voices mingled with laughter came from the kitchen. Herbs and spices filled the air, and Tess didn't know what to think. "What's going on?"

Ethan's concerned expression returned. "Are you okay? Is your head hurting again? You don't remember?"

She shrugged. "I'm as well as I've been all day. What am I supposed to remember?"

"This must be one of those memory lapses the doctors mentioned." Ethan cupped her elbow and guided her toward the noise. At the kitchen doorway, Tess stopped.

Uncle Gordon and Miss Tabitha held sway over three strangers. A blond woman in her midthirties and sporting a lime-green apron sat at the far right end of the table. At the opposite end, a bespectacled man who perched on a stool scratched his hairless head in obvious bewilderment. And between the two, in maroon sweats and sneakers, sat the only person Tess now recognized. Joshua Moore had been Loganton High's track coach for eons. When she walked in, all five sat studying a plucked chicken with trusses unlaced as though enthralled by the sight.

"Tessie!" Uncle Gordon cried when he saw her. "Welcome home. You're just in time. You know Coach Moore, this here's Ann Noonan—she owns the new yarn store downtown. And this one here's Nick Silvestre—just retired from Detroit, and living at The Pines Retirement Community."

The strangers waved.

Tess waved back, bewildered.

Uncle Gordon went on. "Why don't you and Ethan pull up chairs from the dining room and watch Tabby tie up this guy?" He patted one plump, denuded thigh. "He's supper."

Bit by bit, details came to Tess. "That's it!" she finally said. "You and Miss Tabitha are running a cooking school."

"And it's not the kind of thing Tess is up for yet," Ethan said, then turned to Tess. "Would you like me to help you up the stairs?"

As hard as it had been to remember the cooking school, the ease with which memories of the night of the thunderstorm exploded in Tess's head stunned her. She faltered.

Ethan tightened the arm around her waist. "I've got you."

She gave him a weak smile. "I know. Thanks." Then she pulled herself together. "Call me a wimp, but I'd rather stay downstairs. I just remembered the storm." Then, in slow motion, she lifted her foot. "And my foot's still sore."

He took a second to study her face, but then seemed to come to a decision with a nod. "The living room sofa it is, then."

Tess mulled it over. "Actually, if you don't mind, I'd rather go to my office."

"You're not supposed to work for a couple more days."

"I'm not planning to work. I just want to check to see if anything else sold. I don't remember when I scheduled the auctions to close."

He arched a brow. "That, Tess Graver, is what you insist is your current job. I call it work."

"C'mon. It won't hurt to take a quick look."

Ethan led her to the sofa in silence. He seemed to be considering her request. "I'll make you a deal," she said before he had a chance to say no. "I'll let you hide my laptop when I'm done if you give me five minutes to look at my listings. You can be the official keeper of the laptop."

This time he smiled. "If this is your best selling pitch, then you're better off doing business on the Web after all."

He hadn't turned her down—yet. "Just five minutes."

"First you sit." He shook his head. "I know I'm going to regret it, but okay. I'll get you the laptop. And I'll time you, too. Five minutes—not a second more."

As he strolled out of the room, Tess curled up on the

sofa, a fat pillow hugged close to her chest. She loved this house; she always had. After the days she'd spent at the hospital, she welcomed the warmth and memories that surrounded her here, and joy spread from her heart to the very tips of her fingers and toes. She was home. Again.

The chatter in the kitchen made for a pleasant backdrop to her thoughts. Delicious aromas wafted past her, making her mouth water. She eagerly anticipated her first noninstitutional meal, even if it was Uncle Gordon's latest project. All she needed, to make the moment perfect, was to find her listings sold and at a good price.

Another burst of laughter from the kitchen made her smile. Even with a broken leg in a cast, Uncle Gordon was about as impaired as the razor-sharp CEO of a Fortune 500 firm. Cousin Molly could have saved herself the call to Tess. He would have gotten along just fine, Miss Tabitha at his side.

Tess was the one who'd come out on top in that deal. Now that she was home, she doubted she'd ever leave again.

She glanced toward her office. What was taking Ethan so long? "Hey!" she called out in a teasing tone. "Are you checking your e-mail first?"

Seconds later Ethan walked into the living room, laptop in hand, the frown on his forehead again. Her spirits sank.

"What's wrong?"

"I'm sorry, Tess. We're going to have to call Maggie. Someone broke into your office. It's trashed."

EIGHT

Six hours later, as the sun settled below the horizon, Tess sank back into the sofa, exhausted. She heard Maggie Lowe and the other officers and investigators say their goodbyes and the front door close as they left, leaving only silence behind. Tess let out a pent-up sigh.

In the hall Uncle Gordon's walker squeaked to a stop, Miss Tabitha's soft footsteps paused and Ethan's crisp stride came to a standstill. Sibilant whispers reached Tess's ears.

"Hey!" she called, irritated, and none of them had better try to blame her irritation on the knock on the head. She was tired of them using the neurologist's words as an excuse for…whatever. "I didn't lose my hearing. Please come into the living room and tell me what's going on."

The trio walked in, a distinct and different expression on each face. Uncle Gordon looked guilty; Miss Tabitha at peace; and Ethan…well, Ethan's blank stare looked to have taken up permanent residence on his face.

"What were you talking about in the hall?" she asked.

Ethan crossed his arms; Uncle Gordon turned to his lady friend; Miss Tabitha smiled at Tess.

"Honey, you're supposed to rest. Today's been anything but restful. We were keeping quiet so as not to bother you. I'm on my way to clean up after the cooking class."

"Me, too," her uncle said.

Tess had no choice but to accept their explanation. "Okay. Go scrub to your hearts' content."

And then it was just Ethan and Tess in the living room. The grandfather clock in the hall bonged nine times. The expression on her statuelike companion's face never changed.

"My, my," she said, irritated—again. "That's some bedside manner you have there, you bearer of sunshine and cheer, you."

His blue eyes flashed and his jaw tightened. "There's not a whole lot of cheer in a crime spree. Since it seems directed at you, I'm surprised at your…lack of concern, shall we say. You'd better start taking this seriously, Tess. Unless there's something you know and aren't telling us."

Her eyes grew wide. He couldn't have said what she thought he'd said. "I do take it seriously. I have from the start. You didn't really mean that the way it came out, did you?"

A frown lined his brow. "My words stand on their own. You can take them as you wish."

Possibilities ricocheted between the synapses in her brain, and an ugly picture soon formed. "So…let me get this straight. You weren't being a modern-day Good Samaritan back at the hospital, after all, were you?" The sense of betrayal slugged Tess in the gut. How could Ethan even think such a thing about her? "You've been back in agency mode, keeping me under surveillance the whole time. I hope you were good and bored."

His scowl deepened, if possible. "Even you have to admit it's *peculiar* that a rash of crime seems to have followed you home."

"What's peculiar is the rash of crime I stumbled on *after* I got home."

"So, you say you're not involved."

"Absolutely not."

His frown and the tightness of his lips eased a bit. "Okay. Then how about if you tell me how you see the unusual way crime has happened around you?"

She blew a frustrated gust. "I already told you and Maggie. I went jogging, I ran by the woods, wound up getting knocked down by some guy and then I found a woman who died. You can't possibly think I went out there to kill her. I didn't even know her."

If that's what he thinks, then he's certifiably insane.

The pause before he stepped closer spoke louder than when he said in a voice heavy with sadness. "It could be seen as a case of another deal gone bad."

"Ethan! Have you let your bad experiences back in Chicago color everything around you?" Tess couldn't believe what she was hearing. "You saw me that day. I didn't have anything with me to do anyone harm. I didn't even have the means to hide anything in a tank top and running shorts."

The neutral cop face slipped back in place.

"Listen to me," she added. "That woman, according to your own cousin, died of an overdose. What do you think I did? Force her to…to what? I don't know, swallow mountains of meth?"

The blank stare eased into a speculative look. "That wasn't Sarah McVee's manner of death."

To Tess's surprise, he seemed relieved. "Maggie said Sarah died of a methamphetamine overdose. Of course that's the manner of death."

Ethan's shoulders eased a fraction, too. "*Overdose* is the *cause* of death. Manner of death refers to how the overdose came about."

More pieces of the puzzle jelled. Tess's eyes opened wide. "So it was murder! You *do* think I killed her." She gaped. Closed her mouth. Shook her head, but never took her gaze from his. "You're nuts! Totally and completely off the deep end. I don't—didn't—know this Sarah McVee, I know nothing about drug use or abuse, and I would never, ever hurt another human being."

A hint of a smile curved his mouth at her vehemence. "Then you won't mind if the PD looks into every corner of your past."

She laughed. "They can knock themselves out. I don't have a thing to hide. I've never even had a speeding ticket."

Then memories of her troubles at Magnusson's returned. "Oh. Is that it? Did they find out about the thefts at the store?"

That got Ethan's attention like nothing she'd seen before. "Thefts?"

The swift change back to cop mode made the little hairs at the back of her neck stand at attention. A woman had died of a drug overdose, their house had been under siege, she'd nearly been killed, and because of all that, the PD had decided they had reason to suspect Tess.

She was under suspicion.

History did repeat itself.

And history, she hoped, would repeat itself when she proved her innocence. She tipped up her chin. "Yes, thefts. When I worked as a department manager at Magnusson's Department Stores in Charlotte, money began to disappear." In crisp and clear detail, Tess described everything that went down. She detailed the suspicion that had fallen on her, even if had been for a brief time— brief on the calendar, but eternal by how she'd felt.

When she was done, he didn't look convinced—one way or the other. But at least he didn't look like a prosecutor anymore. "Drug use leads to burglaries, holdups, embezzlement—all kinds of theft. The authorities will judge your innocence."

"No, they won't." Tess stood. "Only God can stand in judgment, but they can go ahead and satisfy their curiosity if not their suspicions. And while you're waiting for proof of all I've told you, I suggest you examine the misery you cling to with so much strength, and why you're still clinging to it. Scripture calls us to trust God, leave behind the past and reach forward. I don't see you doing any of that."

He winced but then rearranged his features in the familiar blank stare. "I have a handle on my problems.

I'm sure Maggie will be in touch with the authorities in…was it Charlotte?"

"You know? I can make it easy for them. I'll give you the number to Detective Timmons's direct line at the Charlotte PD. Tell Maggie to ask her everything she wants to know. They can do their worst—or their best. I have a clear conscience."

And a pounding headache to go along with her bruised heart. But there was no reason for Ethan to know about that. Tess crossed her arms and met his gaze with a firm stare of her own.

Toe-to-toe, they stood like two dogs claiming a contested bone. Ethan blinked first.

In a soft voice, he said, "It doesn't look good for you, Tess. To my experienced eye, evidence points to the possibility of another case of no honor among thieves and disagreement among druggies."

Was the man deaf? "I. Told. You. I'd never seen that woman before."

Again, her firm denial seemed to resonate with him. "You know they're going to say you were right there. They might misconstrue your concern and your eagerness to take in a stranger's dog."

Tess gasped. "Oh, no! The dog. I forgot all about him." How could she have done that? Well, there was that knock on the head, but still. "Where is he? Is he okay?"

To her amazement, Ethan blushed, shoved his hands in his pockets and looked away. "Uh…well," he mumbled. "You see…I…took him home with me. He's okay."

Would she ever figure out this man? "You took my dog home with you? To Miss Tabitha's house?"

The red on his cheeks deepened. "I couldn't leave him here by himself. Your uncle's in no condition to look after a dog."

"Dog?" Uncle Gordon asked as he walked into the living room, walker in front, Miss Tabitha two steps behind. "What dog? We don't have a dog for me to look after."

Ethan crossed to the mantel, seemingly fascinated by a jade-green vase. "Actually…"

Miss Tabitha wrung her hands. "Gordon, dear…"

Tess's gaze flew to the floor, the door, the window, the porcelain shepherdess figurine in the curio cabinet against the far wall—anywhere and everywhere but at her uncle's face. "Well…you see…"

Ethan met her gaze. Mischief danced in his eyes. "The ball's in your court, Tess," he said. "And I don't even have a racket to lend you."

She crawled back into her cushy corner of the couch. She'd known this moment would come when she made the decision to take the dog. If it hadn't been for the attempt on her life, it would have happened way before now. Time to pay the piper.

Chin propped on her cushion, Tess stole a look at her uncle and then wished she'd refrained. "Um…you remember the woman I found in the woods, right?"

Through the veil of her eyelashes, she saw her uncle jut out his chin. "Sure. What's she got to do with some mutt?"

Tess offered a silent prayer. "Well, it turns out she had this tiny little dog—the sweetest thing. Two of the officers found it in a carrier in the woods. I couldn't just leave it to die!"

Her uncle's expression turned downright mulish. "I don't cotton to animals living inside people's homes. People are people. Dogs live outside."

She groaned. "Uncle Gordon! If you would only give him a chance. He's tiny and too thin and so, so scared, he could break the hardest heart. Plus he shivers all the time, but he's very, very quiet. You never heard him all the time I had him up in my room."

Her uncle's face turned the color of a cooked beet. "Here? You had a dog here?"

"See?" She tipped up her chin. "He was so good, you never even knew. Give me a chance to prove to you that dogs aren't half-bad."

Miss Tabitha took Uncle Gordon's hand in hers. "I have to tell you, Gordon. This is the saddest little creature. He's been at my place since Ethan brought him the night the van went after Tess, and I've had no trouble from him at all. I think you should give Tess a chance."

"Don't tell me dogs aren't trouble!" Her uncle shook his head. "They chew, they bark, they dig, and then you even have to go around behind 'em with a plastic bag to pick up— No! I don't want a dog."

"You won't have to pick up after him," Tess said. "He's my responsibility." Then she shook her head. "Why do I feel as though I'm back in grade school, Uncle Gordon? I can take care of a dog. Come on. Let me show you."

Ethan turned from the fireplace, an eyebrow raised. "There's another twist to this, Mr. Graver. The dog's evidence. The woman was murdered, and the dog was found at the scene of the crime. Someone's got to look out for him during the investigation."

Uncle Gordon shook his head and aimed his walker toward the hall. "Why don't *you* keep 'im? Your cousin's the cop. That makes more sense."

Ethan looked horrified, and Tess chuckled. "Tell you what?" she asked her uncle. "How about you wait until *after* you meet the dog to decide?"

He paused at the doorway. "And if I still say no, then it's no for good?" Her uncle sent Tess a look of calculation and grit.

Tess let out a big exhale. "Okay. I'll take the risk."

Uncle Gordon and his walker squeaked and clumped out of the room.

Miss Tabitha patted Tess's arm. "I'll be praying for you, dear. I think Gordon'll come around." She crossed to the foyer then opened the front door. "I'll wait for you in the car, Ethan."

Tess considered her situation. Multiple injuries, under suspicion, her new business set back to square one, she sat in the crosshairs of some mystery maniac and now she had to battle her uncle for the sake of an abandoned dog.

She'd always known trial drew a believer closer to God, but the problem about the dog came under the label of nuisance. Ethan's doubts? Those hit hard. True adversity was supposed to reveal a believer's faith, and God, in his great love and mercy, gave believers a choice. She could choose to turn away from God, or she could choose to let her troubles draw her closer to her Lord.

"Tess?" Ethan said.

"Sorry." Her thoughts had drifted and she'd forgotten he was still there. "I was just thinking about…" She made a helpless gesture with her hand.

"I want to make sure you understand. I am helping the Loganton PD with the investigation. But I also want you to know that I hope you're as innocent as you say."

That surprised her. "Thanks."

He chuckled, and while she didn't see much humor, she did see admiration in his expression. "I'll give you this much. You don't back down from a fight."

"Should I?" When he shrugged, she went on. "Here's a news flash, agent man. Neither do you. And until you acknowledge I had nothing to do with Sarah or the break-ins or the van, I won't quit."

He conceded with a nod. "Then you won't object if I stick to you like the proverbial glue."

"Bring it on."

Ethan marched up the ramp to the Graver front porch, the dog's carrier out in front of him. It had taken longer than it should have to get the little beast into its bag. The minute he could put the carrier in Tess's hands wouldn't come soon enough for him.

He let himself in with the key Mr. Graver had given him for the duration of Tess's recovery. In the bright foyer with the tall grandfather clock and walnut console table, he called, "It's me. Where's everyone?"

Mr. Graver helloed from the kitchen, and Tess called out from the sunroom. "I'm at my desk. Come on in."

First things first: unload the dog.

Maggie planned to clear up the issue of the thefts in Charlotte that day. He meant to be with his cousin as she did so. As unprofessional as it was, he clung to the hope Tess's vehement denials last night had given him. He'd never gone into an investigation wanting to find not evidence of guilt but proof of innocence.

He cared for Tess.

The critter in the bag let out a whimper. "Okay," he said. "I get the picture. You're as sick of me as I am of you. Let's get you to your new mommy."

The sunlight that came into Tess's office again made it glow as if lit from within. It struck Ethan as a perfect place to work. No wonder she'd taken over the room for her online auction business.

"Here's your beast," he said, thrusting the carrier farther out.

"And a very good morning—" she glanced at her watch "—by only a bit, to you, too."

When he blushed and mumbled a greeting, she grinned, then said, "Take a good look at what you're calling a beast. He's just a puppy, Ethan. Hardly qualifies as a beast."

He carried the bag to Tess's desk, shaking his head. But before he could make his escape, the down payment on a dog gave a growl. "Easy, Killer," he muttered. "You're home now."

"Killer!" Tess unzipped the carrier door. "That's the most ridiculous thing you could call this dog."

"What do you want me to call a dog who has it in for my toes?"

"What did you do to scare him?" she countered.

Before he could reply, the still-ugly pooch staggered out of the carrier on its toothpick legs. It gave a sniff, then, when it saw Ethan, it went stiff and bug-eyed. Two seconds later it growled again.

"See?" Ethan asked. "I don't have to do a thing. Killer just doesn't like me."

Tess looked from dog to man before scooping up the tiny critter in her arms. The groomer had only improved his looks by a bit. "Don't you think your size and booming voice might scare a bitty thing like…like—"

"Killer." Ethan grinned when she frowned. "He's not that bad. I just wish he wouldn't freak out every time I get close. I took good care of him, and I'm not about to chew him up and spit him out."

"Hey, get a grip, big guy. It's all about six-foot-something versus five-inch-zip."

"Yeah, yeah. And most of the five-inch-zip is fluff." He knew he had her when she fought a smile.

She shot him a mock glare. "The groomer says he'll look better with a good diet, vitamins and regular care of his fur. So you'd better watch it, buster. He's got feelings, you know."

"I think his wacky new owner's the one with the feelings."

"I'll buy that. But you'll have to come up with a better name for him."

"Me! He's not my dog. Thankfully. Tell you what. Why don't you ask your uncle to name him?"

Her smile sagged. "Oh. No, let's not bother Uncle Gordon. He's busy in the kitchen with Miss Tabitha. She got here about an hour before you. That's why I've decided to set up Ki—er...*my dog's* home in my office with me."

"See? I told you Killer's the name. Even your instincts tell you that."

"No way!" Her ponytail swung from side to side, the dark-gold strands threaded through the dark brown catching and dancing in the sunlight. "He's more a Thumbelina type, but he's not a she, so that won't work. You still need a better name."

"Not on your life! Not me."

Something clattered out in the kitchen. The startled dog yipped, growled and then barked up a storm. He took a flying leap from Tess's arms to land catlike on all four tiny paws and then skitter toward the hall.

"Killer!" Ethan called. "Get back here."

Tess went after her pet. "I told you that's not his name. It's, uh, Kibble—no! That's not good, either. Kiwi! That's it. He looks like a kiwi-fruit." She shot Ethan a triumphant look. "Come here, Kiwi!"

Miss Tabitha and Mr. Graver stepped into the sunroom doorway. The dog slid to a full stop inches from the walker's left wheel, eyes bulging, skinny body shaking like a leaf.

Ethan gentled his voice. "Come back here, Killer."

"Kiwi!" Tess wailed. "You have to be good for Uncle Gordon."

"Killer?" Mr. Graver asked, a frown on his usually genial face. "Kiwi?"

"He's not green," Ethan argued, laughter spilling out. "Besides, a runt like him needs a powerful name."

Mr. Graver banged his walker against the floor. "Who you two talking about? What's a killer kiwi?"

Out of the corner of his eye, Ethan saw Tess swallow hard. Then she pointed at her, possibly, pet.

He gestured toward his tiny nemesis, eyes on Tess's uncle.

Miss Tabitha did the same.

Gordon Graver looked down. Ethan knew the moment the older gent realized what he was looking at. Grizzled eyebrows shot up to his thinning hairline. He gaped, and then he, too, pointed at the dog.

"You want me to believe that there…*rat's* a dog?"

Killer, er…Kiwi…*whatever,* stood frozen in place, his eyes like a pair of headlights, his stick legs splayed, his body quivering in terror.

"That, Mr. Graver," Ethan said, "is Tess's new pet. That's her dog."

NINE

So much for professional neutrality. What was it about Tess Graver that had him first spilling his guts and then joking about a dog?

Worse that that. He'd made the biggest mistake of all. He'd set himself up to spend more time under her spell. He'd told her he'd be spending practically every waking minute at her side. Which could prove to be his undoing.

If she was innocent, sure, he'd figure it out. But if she was guilty, he had now provided her with a powerful weapon. He'd given her the chance to watch his every move, too.

So there he sat, on her floral settee in her froo-froo Victorian sunroom office, and with her strange little dog ready to do damage to the tip of his shoes. Mr. Graver had finally scoffed at Killer-Kiwi and given in to the trial period Tess had proposed.

Now, with the dog dilemma resolved, Ethan was about to place an all-important call. When he last spoke to her, Maggie had asked him to handle the detective in Charlotte, since she'd been called to a multi-vehicle accident. He was going to try and learn everything he could about Tess's life in Charlotte. But when he dialed, Detective Timmons wasn't in. He left a voice-mail message, requesting a callback as soon as the detective could manage.

"I guess you'll have to wait for your answers," Tess said when he hung up. "In my experience, she returns calls right away."

Ethan didn't reply; he just shrugged and showed Tess a thick paperback thriller. "I have all the time in the world."

For a moment she looked frustrated, then she turned back to her laptop. After a short burst of furious typing, she sighed and turned on the stereo.

For the next ten minutes or so, Ethan tried without much success to get into his book. But the woman at the desk stole into his concentration with irritating regularity. Each time she slipped into a thought, he forced it aside, refusing to continue the mental duel he'd been having since Maggie had told him the results of the autopsy. He wanted to help solve the murder and he also wanted to find Tess innocent.

But his years at the agency made him fear the worst.

Then Tess pounded her desk. "I'm so sick of this!"

"What's up?" he asked, surprised. "No one's in the urn-buying business today?"

She spun her office chair. "I don't know. I haven't been able to get online—not even last night. By the time you got here, I'd already spent two hours today on the phone with technical support."

"Sounds like trouble. Time to call in a tech whiz."

Tess reached for the phone. "I know, but I can't stand the lost time. I don't want to have potential buyers mad at me because they think I'm unwilling to communicate."

"The sooner you get the computer to the guru, the sooner you'll be back in business."

She nodded, phone to her ear. Ethan returned to his book as she spoke. He found himself reading the same paragraph over and over, and when she was done, he gave up and slapped the paperback shut.

Tess chuckled. "Something on your mind, Mr. Agent Man?"

He narrowed his gaze. "What do you think? I come to Loganton to get away from the devastating results of drug crime, and now I find myself here, keeping an eye on a woman who could be part of that same world."

Instead of losing her temper, she smiled. "I'm sorry."

She sounded almost too sweet. "For what?"

"For wasting your time and all that training. You're barking up the wrong tree with me."

Before he could respond, his cell phone rang. A glance told him it was the call he'd been waiting for. "Hello?"

The conversation lasted less than ten minutes. Detective Marcia Timmons assured him they'd arrested the right woman. Rather than face a trial, the thief had confessed to the scheme, and Tess, who had been under suspicion for a few weeks, was completely exonerated.

As far as any other infractions, the detective assured him Tess's record was cleaner than clean. Ethan felt relief so profound he nearly dropped the phone. He hadn't realized how tense he'd been, how much Tess's innocence mattered to him, and not just as a professional matter.

"Thank you very much for your help," he told the detective.

In her office chair, Tess sat, arms crossed, her smile even wider than before. "Well?"

He blushed. "Well…you were right—"

"Can I have that in writing? And then, do you promise to quit sending me those thundercloud glares?"

Reality returned. He forced his thoughts back along agent lines. "You've only been cleared of theft. Just because your past record is clean doesn't mean you might not want easy money to tide you over until your business begins to turn a profit."

Even as he spoke, Ethan realized the premise was far-fetched at best. He didn't blame Tess for her laugh.

"That is so dumb it makes me wonder what kind of agent you used to be. Not a very good one, I suspect."

That stung. "Okay, so what I said was pretty dumb. But don't doubt my record. I'm proud of what I accomplished during my career, and I have citations and honors to prove my success."

When her eyes narrowed and a sly smile curved her lips, he knew he'd been set up—and he'd fallen for the setup. "Wait—"

"Prove it to me," she said. "Help me find Sarah McVee's killer. Help me prove my innocence. And while you're at it, with all your training, help us track down the monster who's selling meth to Loganton's kids."

The challenge in Tess's gold-and-green eyes was undeniable; the strength of her position, unshakable. And in the end her desire matched his. As reluctant as he'd been at the start, as much as he feared a repeat of the night Robby Stoddard died and as much as the memories still ravaged his sleep, the old drive to find the truth now drove him to act. He wanted her to be innocent.

He stood, his gaze on Tess's fiery eyes. A deep breath settled his anxiety somewhat, and he took the first of a handful of steps he knew would change his life. At her side he held out his hand.

"Tess Graver, you have yourself a deal."

An hour after the handshake Tess knew would change her life, she swallowed a bite of delicious chicken-salad sandwich from last night's cooking class. "Fantastic, Miss Tabitha!"

"She had help," Uncle Gordon teased.

Tess slipped Kiwi, who sat on her lap, a scrap of chicken and winked. "Sure, the three students chopped onions, celery and then stirred mayo into the mix."

"But it was Gordon's special poultry rub we used to begin with," Miss Tabitha said. "That's why the chicken meat tastes so good."

Ethan put down his glass of tea. "A collaborative effort, then."

Tess slanted him a sideways look. "Seems the day for collaboration and cooperation."

"What's that mean?" Uncle Gordon said. "You're not gonna gang up on me again and talk me into another mutt in the house, are ya? Remember. This one's on probation."

She laughed and rubbed Kiwi's little head. "You're safe. Kiwi's my one and only pet."

"You mean Killer," Ethan countered.

"Where's all that cooperation gone?" Uncle Gordon asked, an impish grin on his wrinkled face. "Seems to me the rat's name is Killer Kiwi, even though he's not green."

Instead of continuing the light conversation, Tess turned serious. "Ethan's agreed to help me figure out what's been going on. We've had too many scares, and I'm ready for the siege to be over."

"Help you?" Worry creased Miss Tabitha's brow. "Be careful, Tess. You've had a serious accident."

Tess's resolve only grew. "And I want to prevent any more. I'm not going to do anything stupid, and Ethan assures me—" she sent Ethan a challenging smile "—he's the best the DEA ever had."

"I didn't go that far." His fingers rapped out a brisk rhythm on the tabletop. It caught Kiwi's attention and he stretched his head to peer over the table. He growled at Ethan.

Ethan frowned. "Crazy pooch. Anyway, I am pretty good at what I do, er, what I used to do, *used* to do."

Uncle Gordon turned to Ethan. "So what've you done around here so far?"

Tess didn't know whether to feel sorry for Ethan or to cheer. He squirmed and drew his brows together. "Not enough, sir, obviously—"

"Then what you gonna do about *that?*"

"Well," Ethan said, clearly at a loss, "I have to review the evidence. Then I'll come up with a solid plan."

Pushing away from the table, Tess stood carefully, Kiwi in one arm, waited for the minor light-headedness she'd come to expect to pass and, once it did, took her plate and glass to the sink. "I think Sarah McVee's the key to everything. I'm sure even the phone calls and the break-ins are tied to her death."

Ethan conceded with a nod. "I have to agree, and I need to get with Maggie to see what she has on Miss McVee. But when we last spoke, she said she'd be in court this afternoon, to testify in a drunk-and-disorderly. She'll call me when she's done."

The doorbell rang. Tess hurried to greet the computer tech. "I'm so happy to see you."

The squat young man, a pen over his left ear, his white shirt and gray pants ill fitting and wrinkled, shrugged. "That's what everyone says. Show me the machine."

Tess led him to her office, Ethan at her heels. She glanced over her shoulder, noting his stare fixed on the young man ahead. Poor guy. That laser gaze could make the most innocent person squirm.

After Stan, the computer whiz, fiddled with her laptop, turning it over, opening covers in the back, typing, checking the various USB ports and all the cords, he turned to Tess. "This is gonna take some time, so…maybe you can…oh, go chill."

At her back, Ethan laughed. "In other words," he whispered, his breath blowing a wisp of hair against Tess's cheek, "'get out of my hair.'"

The strongest urge to lean back against his strength overtook her. But she couldn't do that. All they had between them was a fragile truce.

She didn't know if he wished there were more.

Like she did.

She shook herself. "Um…we'll leave you to your work." When she turned, she found herself inches from Ethan's chest. She drew in a deep breath.

The fleeting urge to lean on him returned, this time with much more intensity. Experience had taught Tess how strong Ethan was, and even though she tried to put up a courageous front for her uncle and Miss Tabitha, she was no fool. Someone was out to hurt her, maybe worse, and since her head injury, she felt too weak to put up a good enough fight.

When Ethan didn't pull back, Tess let her gaze wander up his navy-blue knit shirt to his neck, the strong muscles well delineated, past his square jaw, lips and straight nose to snag on his blue stare. A touch of surprise lightened his usually serious expression. He raised a hand, slipped a lock of hair behind her ear, his blue eyes staring into hers. As unlikely as it might be, Ethan seemed as affected by their nearness as she.

"Achooo!"

"Grrr!"

The computer tech's sneeze and Kiwi's response brought Tess back out of the spell Ethan's nearness put on her. "Ah. We'll be in the living room or the kitchen. That is, if you need me for, well, for questions. The computer's still under warranty."

From under the cover of her lashes, she watched Ethan's expression slowly change. He'd never taken his gaze from her, but now a smile, the real deal, curved his lips. She hadn't fooled him. He knew the effect he'd had on her.

She could barely breathe. Did it mean…?

No! It meant nothing. Just that he'd caught her admiring his admittedly good looks. So sue her.

He'd said he hoped she was innocent. As long as any doubt lingered in his mind, she couldn't let his appeal grow. She'd suffered through others' suspicions enough.

But it was way past time to get a grip on her wandering thoughts. "Let's go," she said in her crispest voice.

In the hall, however, Tess tried to come up with a reason to send Ethan packing, to escape from the draw of his appeal. But if she did, he was sure to think she'd gone off the deep end: she'd just performed major mental gymnastics to get him to agree to work with her.

So what did she really want?

Maybe she had gone off the deep end after all. She was having a hard time stringing thoughts together so they made sense. She wandered into the foyer, ideas racing in her head.

Ethan took his time, which gave Tess the opportunity to cobble up a plan. When he met her by the grandfather clock, without looking past the top button of that navy blue shirt, she said, "I can't stand to just sit here and wait for the creep who's been after me to strike again. I want to do something—anything—to avoid another assault."

"What do you want to do? The PD's doing a good job with the investigation."

"I know they are. Plus you're here, kind of like a self-appointed bodyguard, and I appreciate your help, but you are an investigator." She hated the pleading note in her voice; she'd reached the end of her rope. She couldn't just wait around for the next shoe to drop. "Investigate. Help me figure it out."

"I told you I had to wait for Maggie—"

"You may have to wait to see what the cops have, but has it occurred to you to just…I don't know, follow up, maybe? Check things out? Maybe your experience will help you pick up something the officers missed."

When Ethan began to shake his head, Tess's sense of urgency grew. "Have you learned anything about Sarah McVee? Who was she? Where did she come from? What did she do? When did she move to town? And what about the other meth overdoses? Who were they, really? Is there a connection between them?"

As she shot her barrage of questions at him, conflicting emotions flitted across his face. In the end, Tess identified that recurring touch of admiration and this time a lot of concern. "The underbelly of the drug trade is a dangerous place to be," he finally said. "Someone from that world just tried to take you out. You were lucky. You're just out of the hospital. Don't be in such a hurry to return."

"I don't intend to return to the hospital, but I also refuse to become one of those famous sitting ducks. I want to figure this all out, and we can start by learning everything there is to know about Sarah McVee."

The blue eyes narrowed and a tight smile curved Ethan's lips. "We don't have the authority to do that. How do you plan to go about your information gathering?"

Plan? She hadn't thought far enough ahead to come up with a plan. He was supposed to be the ace investigator.

But she was the one pushing for action.

"Uh...okay! I want to see where she lived." That was something TV cops always did.

Ethan seemed to relax. "You don't have to do that. The PD already processed the place."

"But *you* didn't."

She'd surprised him. "You're right. I've only consulted with the investigators on this case. That's all they've asked for. Remember, I'm not in law enforcement any more."

"You used to be. This is what you once did, and you know what to look for—maybe even better than our cops."

When Ethan didn't respond, Tess marched to the front closet, opened the door, yanked out her purse, looped it over her shoulder and faced Ethan again. "Coming with me? I'm off to find out who Sarah McVee was."

Ethan swallowed hard. A haunted look appeared in his eyes. He fisted his hands, and in profile he looked carved from stone.

As Tess studied him, understanding dawned. Ethan hadn't let himself move past the drug bust in the alley. Not only had he been affected by what he saw at the scene of a horrible crime, but he'd also made it the defining moment of his life. He'd fled his former career, and looking into Sarah McVee's past reminded him too much of his own pain, much more than skimming his cousin's notes at the PD or a simple call to a Charlotte detective or even babysitting Tess.

Sympathy made her waver, but then the memory of something she'd told him returned: she'd urged him to examine the misery to which he clung with so much fervor, and his reason for clinging. She'd also reminded him that Scripture calls believers to trust God, to leave behind the past and reach forward.

To a lesser degree, she'd done that when she'd chosen to leave a bad situation in Charlotte and get on with her life back home. True, Robby Stoddard's death didn't compare with being suspected of a crime she didn't commit, but it looked as though Ethan couldn't leave his past behind; he might even be coasting in neutral instead of reaching forward.

Would it help him if she gave him a nudge? Would he confront the memories that clearly haunted him? Would he then get on with his life?

And then what?

A niggling twinge scratched at her conscience. Were her motives pure? Or did she secretly hope a healed Ethan would turn to her?

Worse yet, was she trying to take over God's job? Only God should handle Ethan's heart. Only God knew what was best for Ethan. Her meddling might make matters worse.

Ugh! How awful. That possibility said nothing good about Tess. She breathed a quick plea for forgiveness and asked the Lord to continue to reveal His plan for her life. She also prayed for protection, insight and guidance as they looked into the attacks. She couldn't be wrong in wanting to know who was targeting her and why. Right?

Only after she—and the police—knew, would it all stop.

She pushed aside her feelings for Ethan, squared her shoulders and met his gaze. "Do you know where Sarah McVee lived?"

He hesitated a moment. "There's only one cheap motel close enough to town. Of course I know where she lived."

Tess let Stan know of her change in plans, and he agreed to tell Uncle Gordon the computer's diagnosis and prognosis before taking off. Then she turned to Ethan again.

"Let's go crank up your metal steed and get on our way."

Seconds later, before Ethan could stop her, Tess grabbed the paper anchored by his wiper blade. He leaned close and they both read the threat.

"Last chance. Give it back."

Her fingers shook. The paper shivered. Ethan met Tess's gaze, and instead of fear, he saw rage, righteous rage. It matched the anger in his gut. Certainty began to grow.

Tess didn't deserve this. She had done nothing wrong. The police had found no evidence against her, and he no longer needed it. In his heart he knew the truth.

"I'll take you to Sarah McVee's room after we seal that note in a plastic bag."

She arched a brow. "Partners?"

"To the end."

Fifteen minutes later, when Tess walked past Ethan as he held the motel's front door open, she had the sense of stepping onto the set of a bad B movie. The place was dark and drab. Heavy drapes in the shade of an overcast sky obscured any light that might otherwise filter through the windows she'd seen from outside. A Formica-topped counter filled a corner at the back-left side of the room, and a bank of wooden cubbies rose to fill the wall behind that. As Tess moved closer to Ethan's side, a frowsy woman behind the desk yelled into the phone.

"I toldja not to take that there fancy-pants job, girl," she said. "You had it good with me here."

The late-forties woman's mouse-brown hair had been frosted blond so long ago that the wiry strands looked in need of a good dusting, like the rest of the place. Frameless glasses bobbed on the bridge of her nose, and her thin lips pursed in disgust. Narrow, hunched shoulders finally shrugged. A tarnished name tag identified her as Carla.

"It's your funeral, girl. Don't know if I'm willing to give ya yer job back." She slammed the phone into its base.

For the girl's sake, Tess hoped she found greener employment pastures elsewhere. "Hi," she said, her friendliest smile pasted on her face.

Before she could say another word, Ethan stepped up

to the counter. "I'm assisting the Loganton PD with their investigation into Sarah McVee's death," he said.

Suspicious brown eyes peered through her specs. "That's very, very interesting. Cops were here a coupla days ago. Now you're telling me you're working with 'em. How'm I gonna know that's true?"

"I'll be happy to wait until you call Officer Maggie Lowe. She's in charge of the case."

The clerk weighed his words. "But you're not a cop."

Ethan took a breath so deep it raised his shoulders significantly. "My experience is with the DEA—Drug Enforcement Agency." His voice came out rougher than usual, but not as harsh as when he'd told Tess about the bust gone bad. "The coroner determined that Sarah died of an overdose—"

The woman's gaunt, freckled cheeks reddened. "My motel's a clean place. I don't cotton to no drug selling here. And you uppity busy-nosies aren't gonna tell me my lodgers are what they ain't."

Tess bumped up against Ethan's arm. The woman protesteth too much.

"No one has suggested that," Ethan said. "We're trying to learn as much as possible about Miss McVee. Who were her friends? What kind of work did she do? Where did she spend her free time?"

"I don't stick my nose in my guests' business. Can't answer none of that." Then Carla narrowed her eyes and crossed her thin arms. "I figure this means she went and got herself knocked off."

"That's a strong possibility." Ethan leaned on the

counter, looking far more relaxed than Tess felt. "I'd like to look around her room. I know the police came by, but I like to see things myself. I'm sure you understand."

Wiry hair bounced up and down. "Don't I know it! I want something done, gotta do it myself." She narrowed her gaze. "It still don't feel right, you two nosing in that room."

"I see." Ethan headed for the door, but then he paused. "Maybe you can answer a question. I was thinking…did she ever have friends stop by?"

The clerk lifted a shoulder. "Dunno. I never spy on my guests."

Ethan pressed on. "Any calls? Messages?"

Carla huffed out a long-suffering sigh. "Some guy did call every once in a while. But I put his calls through and didn't listen to no conversations. Carla Rheining ain't that kind of woman."

Ethan pushed away from the counter. "The thought never crossed my mind. Do you know if he ever picked her up? Did he visit?"

"I'll have you know, mister, I don't cotton to immoral behavior on my premises. My property's who I am."

Tess traded a glance with Ethan. So Carla owned the motel. No wonder she was so defensive.

"And I commend you," Ethan answered. "But I don't think someone picking up someone else is especially immoral."

The clerk sniffed. "You might be right about that."

Ethan leaned on the counter again. "Can you try to remember? It's important."

"I can try." Carla removed her glasses, pinched the bridge of her nose and tightened her eyes. "Hm…ya know? I think some man came to meet her here one time—in the parking lot, not inside."

"When?" Ethan asked.

"When?" Tess asked.

They traded looks, then turned to Carla. "Oh… mighta been about a month ago, maybe two."

Ethan prodded. "What kind of car did he drive? What did he look like?"

"Whaddaya think I am?" She donned her frameless specs and, after a brief silence, said, "I didn't see him drive up. She didn't have a car, neither. Didn't have the money, she said."

"Did she work?" Tess asked, bracing for Ethan's glare, which, thankfully, didn't come.

"Beats me," Carla said. "She paid late but she paid. She's paid up through the end of the month. That's why I haven't cleaned out the room yet."

Tess pressed. "Can you remember anything about the man?"

"Don't think he had red hair. I would have remembered that. They didn't stick around long, neither, so I didn't get a good gander at him."

"We understand," Ethan said. "Could you answer just another question or two?"

"Two. No more'n two more. I got things to do."

Tess looked around the lobby. When she faced the motel owner again, Carla had the grace to blush. "Two questions, then go bug someone else."

"What do you remember about the man? It could be important."

"He wasn't tall, but he wasn't short," Carla said. "He wasn't fat, either. I'd've noticed. And he left with Sarah McVee."

"How long did Sarah live here?" Ethan asked.

"'Bout four months."

He frowned. "And in all that time you never asked her what she did? Where she worked?"

"Hey!" the motel owner objected. "I agreed to two questions, and that's a whole bunch more. I don't know where she worked, but she was always dressed up fancylike, smelled good and had her hair all done up nice. Looked like something one of Monique's girls might have done. Maybe she sold clothes in a store or maybe she did people's hair herself."

"So, did you decide to let us see the room?" Tess held her breath.

TEN

Carla sighed, dipped below the top of the counter and then bobbed back up again. She held out the key. "But I better not find that there room any worse than it is after you're gone. Carla Rheining ain't no fool, you know."

"Of course not." Ethan took the key. "We only want to look around. We'll leave everything the way it is."

After thanking her, they headed back out and down the walkway to room number eighteen. "Ethan," Tess whispered. "Sarah couldn't have been dealing drugs if she lived in a place this shabby."

The look he sent her would have quelled a riot. "Not now! Don't say anything else."

Once in the room, Tess looked around, stunned by what she saw. Chaos reigned from wall to wall. The pillows on the bed had been ripped. The filling made clouds across the naked mattress, and some spilled over the edge, since the whole bed had been moved. Hills and valleys of dirty laundry littered the floor. Jars of creams and lotions and a makeup case on the small vanity outside the bathroom door had been emptied, the contents of the beauty products melding into a gelatinous ooze. The bathroom itself spoke volumes about Carla's cleaning crew, none of it good. It also said a lot about Sarah McVee's drug addiction.

And it said someone had ransacked the place before the cops got to it. Smudges from police fingerprint dust streaked every visible surface.

The steel rack that doubled as a closet to the right of the vanity held one warped wire hanger and, while the dresser drawers were closed, Tess suspected they were similarly empty. She opened the top one and, sure enough, found nothing inside.

"See anything?" she asked Ethan. "Any drug paraphernalia?"

He turned slowly, his blue eyes touching on every detail in the room. "Maggie and her guys would have taken that as evidence. Aside from the mess, I see nothing here."

"Then let's not waste more time."

As Ethan closed the door, Tess figured out what had teased her mind in the room. "How sad! I didn't see any dog food or bowls or toys."

"Someone with a habit like Sarah McVee's wouldn't think about much more than the drug. Killer's meals must have been a hit-or-miss deal."

"Kiwi," she corrected automatically. Then anger bubbled up. "Let's go *do* something about whoever's making…selling—whatever—this stuff."

Ethan arched a brow then grinned. "Any more ideas?"

"Don't tease! You're the expert here."

His eyes twinkled. "But you're all fired up."

That was true. "Let's go hit the salon. Carla mentioned that Sarah's hair always looked nice. Women talk when they get their hair or nails done and there's only one place in town to do that, Monique's Mane Management."

"Okay, okay." He dangled the room key. "Let me return this, and we'll be on our way. Monique's Mane Management, here we come."

Tess waited by the SUV, basking in the spring sunshine. In spite of her new partner's reluctance, she was gaining insight into an Ethan Rogers she hadn't known, one she suspected few people knew. The more she learned about him, the more she found to like.

"Ready?" he asked as he unlocked the car.

"And rarin' to go." Inside, she clicked on her seat belt then turned to him. "You know—"

Suddenly the rear window of the SUV shattered into a million little pieces.

Maggie grilled them for an hour or more. Now his cousin was peppering Tess with even more questions. He'd told Maggie all he knew; so had Tess. They didn't know much. They'd come to see Sarah McVee's room and hadn't learned much more than they already knew. Then, when they were about to leave, someone had used Ethan's SUV for target practice. Thankfully, no one was hurt. This time.

"Hey, Mags," he said as his cousin closed her notepad. "You do realize that even though the perp put

Tess in the hospital, he could have killed her—twice now. He's been holding back."

"She has something he wants." Maggie glanced at Tess, who sat on the curb in front of Sarah's motel room, arms hugging herself tight. "And I doubt she has a clue what it might be. Unless she's been putting on an Oscar-worthy performance, I don't think Tess Graver's involved."

He grinned. "Glad you agree."

Maggie crossed her arms and studied him in silence. "What…?"

"So are you in? Are you going to give it your best shot, and help us nail this creep?"

His slow nod came easier than his agreement with Tess had. "Now, how do we get back home? You've impounded my car. I can walk, but Tess can't."

"Sorry about that. You know how it goes—it's evidence." She bobbed her head toward her partner. "Wayne's going to drive you. We already talked."

"Can he bring me up to speed on the way?"

Maggie snorted. "We don't have much more than what you already know. That's the problem. We're dealing with a pro."

An uneasy feeling settled in Ethan's stomach as he went over to Tess. "Hey." He wrapped an arm around her shoulders. "Ready to go? Maggie's partner, Wayne is going to drive us home."

She shrugged, and her lukewarm response told Ethan more than words. Just when his resolve was growing stronger, she was letting discouragement steal hers. He couldn't let it happen. That's when the perp would come in for the—

He wasn't going there. He gave her a little squeeze. "Come on. Let's go. We still have a date with Monique."

When she met his gaze, he read fear in her eyes. "I wish I knew what he wanted. I'd be more than happy to give it back."

"That wouldn't stop the flow of drugs," he said, determined to fire her up again. "We have to get to the bottom of this, not just give him what he wants."

"What if he's too smart? What if he's committed the perfect murder? What's to keep him from doing it again? I have to protect Uncle Gordon."

"The best way to do that is to flush him out of his cave."

She exhaled and her shoulders slumped. "What if—"

"Let me get this straight. You fast talk me into jumping into this investigation, get me going, and now, when I'm ready to roll, you want to back out? What's this? A case of fair-weather courage?"

Her back straightened as if he'd stuck her with a pin. "No, but—"

"This isn't the time for buts." What he was about to say was going to scare her, but he hoped it scared her into action. Now that he was in, he was in to win. "That bullet tells me the perp's getting desperate. This is when he starts to make mistakes. We're close, and we can't back down now, not when he's gone so far as to pull a gun. And you can believe he'll keep that gun handy until he gets what he wants."

"Or until we bring him down."

"Now you sound like yourself again. I thought I'd lost the real Tess for a moment there."

"Hey!" Wayne yelled. "You two coming?"

They rode in silence. At the Graver home, they said goodbye to Maggie's partner, and, as they went up the ramp to the front porch, Tess patted the handrail. "Have I thanked you lately for this thing?"

"You and your uncle have thanked me plenty."

"I don't know what we would have done without it. Even after he gets his walking cast, Uncle Gordon is going to have a hard time with stairs. You're one of the good guys."

Ethan shrugged. "It didn't take a long time, and Joe and I work well together. Besides, your uncle's great. Who wouldn't want to help him?"

Tess opened the door. "Speaking of my uncle…" She gave a yell. "Anybody home?"

When her words echoed in the silence, Ethan had a momentary pause. Had anything happened while they were gone? Tess's gaze mirrored his concern.

"Don't worry," he said. "Let's check things out—"

"Oh, look!" She waved a torn page from a notebook. "They left this—a good note this time. Miss Tabitha drove them to the seniors' center. He wanted to watch this afternoon's film. And they took the dog!"

"I told you he'd come around once he got to know your mutt. They'll be best friends by tonight." Ethan grinned. "Mr. Graver's something else. Not much gets him down, does it?"

Tess chuckled. "He's a force unto himself." She

pointed to the note. "He says Stan fixed the laptop. *I* say it better stay fixed longer than the last time." For a moment she looked torn. "I know we need to find this creep before he strikes again, but I also need to check the items I put up for sale days ago."

Ethan glanced at his watch. "Go ahead, but don't take too long."

This smile was the most natural she'd given him since the shooting took place. "I won't take long. I don't have that many listings yet."

A series of clicks later, she cheered. "I sold the microwave! Oh, and Uncle Gordon's goofy key-chains went, too."

"So how's the urn-selling business these days?"

She scrolled down a line or two. "Yep. The second one went—and for more than the first. I might really be on to something with these urns."

"Don't tell me you're going to specialize in them."

"No, but I won't turn them down, either." She powered down the machine, clicked it shut, patted it and then stood. "On to Monique's. Since you're fresh out of wheels, I'll drive us there in style."

Ethan winced. The powder-blue Cadillac wouldn't have been his first or even his tenth choice, but Tess wasn't well enough to walk downtown yet. Plus he could do a better job keeping her safe at his side than if she stayed home on her own. Her company gave him the determination to press on, to get beyond the reluctance his memories had forged. Her smile broke through the dark moods and his sense of failure, and her plight tugged at his heart, a heart that had found a place for Tess.

"I'll do the driving. The neurologist hasn't cleared you yet." He ignored her scowl.

In the car Ethan went on. "Don't get too excited about the hairdresser. I doubt Sarah would have told her about her drug problems or who supplied her, and where she got the money to pay for her hair care."

"True. But some women tell their hairdressers more than they should without realizing what they've said— or how many others might have heard."

"You don't think Maggie's guys got the hairdresser to talk?"

"Only if Carla mentioned the hair angle to them. And it depends on the hairdresser. How she feels about her client—and cops. My questions might not be the same ones they asked. Besides I don't look or sound like a cop."

He arched a brow.

Tess went on. "Sarah might have mentioned getting ready for a special date or grumbled if they had a fight. Salons are major male-bashing pits."

He shot her a disgusted glare. "Which is why I can't believe I let you rope me into this. If Carla mentioned the salon, I'm sure the police asked the hairdressers whether Sarah ever talked about anyone. I doubt we'll get anywhere here. Not in a—what'd you call it? Oh, yeah. A male-bashing pit."

She grinned. "Oh, you might catch something I miss."

"I'm sure I've had more fun at my dentist's office."

"This isn't about fun," Tess said. "It's about finding Sarah's killer."

Ethan clicked on the signal and made a smooth turn. "You're right. But consider this. Sarah probably wasn't just an addict. She was probably a courier of some sort. She could pay for her room—erratically, but she paid—and salon visits."

"That makes sense." Then Tess frowned. "But why kill her? What would make a courier no longer useful?"

Tess waited for her answer while Ethan parallel parked in front of the salon. "Well?"

"She was a user, Tess. She probably helped herself to the merchandise. Or she might have made off with a wad of cash. Or she might have threatened to quit and go get clean. I don't know."

She gave him a knowing look. "But you're going to find out."

"You got it."

Then Ethan drove right past the salon. "Whoa!" Tess cried. "Where are you going? Monique's is back there."

"This is a small town, and everyone knows your uncle's car. After that shot today, I'm not inviting another one by parking right on Main Street."

"You really think that madman would shoot at us twice in one day?"

He pulled into the alley behind the Main Street shops. "There's nothing drug dealers won't do. I'm not giving him any invitations." He parked behind a green dumpster, then opened his door. "Let's go."

When they stepped into the salon, Ethan began to

squirm. Tess grinned. The über-feminine lavender establishment didn't cater to males, so she gave him a break and took the lead when the young woman with bright fuchsia hair at the front desk glanced up.

"I'd like to talk to Sarah McVee's stylist," Tess said.

The pink-haired beauty blew and popped a matching gum bubble. "You need *him* along to check out a stylist?"

"I can talk to a stylist on my own, but we're not here about me. This is about Sarah McVee."

"The chick who died the day Mandy put in some highlights, right?"

Tess's impatience made an appearance, but she knew she couldn't get on the gatekeeper's bad side. "If Mandy's the one who did Sarah's hair, then that's who I want to see. According to her landlord, Sarah was a regular here."

The girl opened her schedule book. "I can see if she always saw Mandy…"

"Is Mandy in today?" Tess asked.

With a shrug, the girl pointed into the salon. "Over there, with the lady soaking her feet for a pedicure. You can talk to her, but just let her keep doing her thing. She might get in trouble with the owner if she falls behind because of you."

Ethan snagged her elbow before Tess could take a step. "I'm skipping this one."

She just gave him a mischievous wink.

As Tess approached, Mandy rolled yet another lock of the older lady's silver hair onto a pink perm rod. But when Tess asked about Sarah, Mandy had little to say. Sarah hadn't been talkative, and even though Mandy had done something new to Sarah's hair every two weeks or so, they'd remained strangers for the most part. Mandy described Sarah as her most boring client.

When Mandy snapped shut the last one in a row of about twenty pink rods, Tess remembered the mystery man Carla Rheining had mentioned. "Did Sarah ever bring her friends to get their hair done here? You do a great job."

Mandy shook a bottle of cloudy liquid. "Sarah brought her dog, but she never brought friends. She said she didn't know anyone in town yet."

"I've just come back to town, and while I was gone, I lost track of a lot of my friends, so I can understand." Every squirt of the acrid-smelling potion stung Tess's nose; she couldn't wait to leave. But there was so much they needed to know. "So did she date a lot? Did you ever see her with a cute guy? You know, like, did he ever drop her off? Or maybe walk her here. Did he pick her up after her appointments?"

Mandy sniffed. "I don't spy."

Different woman, same response. "I didn't think you did. I heard she had a…special friend, a guy. I just wondered if you'd seen him."

"D'you mean her cousin? She did say she was meeting him the last day she was in. But I never saw him."

Tess's heart sped up. "Did she tell you his name?"

"Nah. Just that they were getting together, and she wanted to look her best. We even did her makeup, but it didn't do much good. Poor thing, her skin was a mess."

"Was her cousin visiting from out of town? Or does he live around here?"

"How should I know? All Sarah said was he liked her to look businesslike. I asked what kind of work she did, but she just said she worked for him."

Tess fought down her excitement. "Thanks, Mandy. You've really helped."

A pretty brunette knelt by the foot-soak basin at Mandy's client's feet. "Excuse me."

Mandy grinned. "No prob, Angie." Then Mandy turned back to Tess. "Glad I could help, but what did I help you with?"

"Sarah was doing drugs, and he—" she pointed toward the waiting area "—has DEA connections."

Mandy's eyes widened. "So that's why her skin was such a mess! And her teeth? Oh, she was always complaining about a toothache. Drugs'll ruin your looks faster'n anything else."

Tess scrambled for another question. "Oh! How about her little dog? Did her cousin give it to her?"

"She never said much about the dog, but she always brought him in a cute little carrier."

"You're sure you don't remember *anything* else about the cousin?"

The nail tech glanced up. "I don't like to talk about my clients, but I did Sarah's manicure all the time. That last day, she said something about her cousin, that he was a tough boss, and that he had something to do with the government. She said she always did what he asked, since he took good care of her, but she sounded scared to me. Sarah was strange."

She was getting somewhere! "Did you see the cousin?"

Angie wrapped the fascinated senior citizen's foot in a lavender towel. "Not that day, but she did meet a guy out front a couple of weeks ago."

Tess resumed her girly talk. "What did he look like? Was he cute?"

Angie shot her a penetrating look. "I don't like this, okay? I don't talk about my clients, but you said it had to do with cops, the DEA and drugs." She treated her client's other foot to a matching towel. "He was maybe medium height—not tall. He had big shoulders, too. Oh! And I think he had dark hair."

Tess couldn't wait to tell Ethan what she'd learned. "Thank you, Angie. You've been great." She turned to Mandy. "Sarah had beautiful hair. You did a terrific job for her. I'm going to make an appointment, and maybe you can do something as nice for me."

Fighting the urge to hurry, to do something, to track down the man, Tess made herself put foot before foot and stroll to the waiting room. There she tapped Ethan, who was reading an old copy of a news magazine. "We're done."

As soon as the salon door closed behind them, Tess grabbed his arm. "Ethan! You're not going to believe what I learned." In a rapid-fire rush, she brought him up to speed, especially about Sarah's cousin. "Well? What do you think?"

Ethan's expression had darkened as she talked. "I don't think he was her cousin, and I don't like any of it. That 'cousin' sounds too familiar. Drugs, a dead contact."

"Someone you busted before?"

"They're all the same."

As soon as she realized his thoughts had turned to the back alley in Chicago, she released his arm. Two steps put a modest distance between them, and while she was willing to respect his pain and give him space, she didn't have the luxury to let him regress.

"But, Ethan, that description could fit thousands of men. Why would you think of that…that Moreno guy. And here in Loganton?"

He headed for their car. "The difference between Moreno and the thousands of other guys is the drugs and the death. Ernesto Moreno has an empire that spreads across a number of states, and he casts a long shadow in my memory."

"This isn't Chicago, L.A. or New York. We're talking the boondocks, here. You can't be so paranoid to think he'd follow you here?"

After unlocking the car, Ethan flicked up her lock. "I suppose you're right. I couldn't tell you what Moreno's up to or how far his tentacles might spread. I do know he got started in the early nineties, and, even though he still calls the shots, over the years he's set up pals in more states than I want to count." He shrugged. "I don't know that he has anymore this far in the east but anything's possible. Sarah was the kind of person he liked to use."

"I don't know… Angie the nail tech said Sarah's cousin had a government job."

"That doesn't mean much. It's a cover, Tess. I'm sure this guy has had dozens of jobs over the years."

Ethan turned the key, and a blast of hot air slapped Tess in the face. "It's still a place to start."

Backing up, he shook his head. "We don't have a name to trace—you don't think her killer used the real one, do you? We don't even think Moreno used his real name. Who knows who this guy really is?"

Her earlier excitement took a hit. "Then what's next?"

"The two other victims. I want Maggie's files. She doesn't think there's a connection between them, but I'm not a coincidence kind of guy."

As he drove, Ethan prayed. *Is this my second chance, Lord? It sure feels like Moreno all over again. And You know I'd like nothing more than to nail people like him. I couldn't save Robby back then, Father, but will You help me find justice for the addicted people in Loganton? And help me keep Tess safe.*

His cell phone rang, breaking into his prayer. "Maggie! What's up?"

"Come meet me at the Newmans' place. When the three sons went to take down an old shed at the back of the property this morning, they found it had burned down, probably while the parents wintered down south. I think we found the meth lab."

ELEVEN

Tess had refused to stay in the car while Ethan viewed the remains of the lab. She'd pleaded, and Ethan had gone to bat for her. Eventually Maggie had agreed to let her go, under the condition that Tess wear protective gear and let Maggie and Ethan take the lead.

Tess had no trouble wearing the Tyvek splash suit Maggie handed her, but she did question the need for the respirator that looked like a bug's head. "Why do we need these? We're out in the open."

Ethan pulled an identical gadget over his head. "The contamination at even an abandoned meth site can last for years, and it will damage your eyes and lungs," he said, his voice muffled by the mask. "That's why cleanup's such a complicated process. The soil's a mess, and sometimes the authorities wind up razing the place."

"That's good enough for me." Tess pulled on the confining mask. "But why knock down the place? Can't you just get rid of the stuff, and then clean up and sanitize what's left?"

"Sometimes you can, but the fumes from the cookers seep into everything, and they sometimes can't be cleaned. Drywall and wood, even wall studs become so saturated that pregnant women who live in contaminated places have had babies with birth defects. Anyone exposed to that devil's brew will wind up with some kind of permanent damage."

Her opinion of the awkward suit shot way up. "I'll never understand why people choose to use drugs."

"They have a million reasons, Tess, but it's always complicated."

When Ethan held out a hand to help her over the split-rail fence, Tess hung tight. But when she tugged to pull away, he tightened his clasp. She met his gaze through their lenses, read his request. She nodded, happy to trust his expertise.

They followed Maggie to the charred remains of the shed. When Ethan had told Tess about the meth lab the Newmans' sons had found, she'd expected something with high-tech gadgets and obscure ingredients. What she saw shocked her.

The fire had blazed unevenly. The left side of the shed had become a line of ashes and blackened wood. Empty containers of lye, drain cleaner, a can of Toluene, dozens of glass beakers, a tangle of melted plastic tubing, and a crushed box of Epsom salts lay strewn along what once was the back wall. Near what must once have been the door, Tess saw two gas cans, a five-gallon plastic container of pool chemicals—empty and on its side—and a pile of scorched rags, red and yellow stains still visible on the parts that hadn't burned. Old rechargeable batteries dotted the mess.

"What do you think?" Maggie asked Ethan. "An explosion or did they try to burn the evidence?"

"There's no way to tell for sure. All this stuff—" he gestured "—is flammable, so when you test, your results will always show chemical accelerants."

"Any hope they might have left the area? Or do you think they set up shop somewhere else?"

"They probably left when the Newmans came back, and they're somewhere cooking up more of this stuff. They need the goods to make the bucks."

Maggie sighed. "Seen enough? I don't want to hang around here, even in the suits, any longer than we have to. The Haz-Mat guys from Charlotte should be here soon. They're better equipped to handle this than we are. I'll make sure they know you want to meet with them."

Ethan took another look at the wound on the earth. "Yeah, I'm done. I have to make a couple of calls."

Tess had seen enough, too. They had a creep—or maybe more—to find before he struck again. And they wouldn't find him in the Newmans' back field.

Ethan tugged on her hand.

Tess didn't need another invitation. She matched her steps to his as they headed toward the split-rail fence, Maggie at their side.

"Tell me about those calls you want to make, cuz," the petite officer said.

Ethan's already broad shoulders looked massive when he shrugged inside the splash suit. "I want to check in with Steve. I want to know whether this guy's a lone entrepreneur or if one of the bigger drug lords has spread his operation and set up satellites in the Carolinas."

"Oh, come on, Ethan," Maggie countered, taking off her mask. "That's a stretch. Moreno can't be everywhere. What would major dealers be doing here?"

Tess removed her respirator to reveal her grin. Her point, precisely.

Ethan narrowed his gaze behind the plastic lens. "For example, by the time we'd cornered Moreno, we'd tracked his accomplices across eighteen states, Mags. Most of these guys have been at this since the nineties, okay? Who knows how far their networks really reach? We can't just ignore this."

Maggie crossed her arms, the mask dangling from a hand. "Do you know anything I don't know to point us in that direction?"

Ethan tugged off his respirator then tipped his head toward Tess. "I don't know if we have anything, but you can ask her. She's the ace who got the goods."

Tess described their visit to Monique's.

"Oh, this is bad," Maggie said. "I can't believe a civilian learned more than we did. I'll have to deal with my guys, and then face the chief for the fallout."

Ethan paused in the process of removing his splash suit. "So you're going to ignore the possibility this guy's part of something bigger? Are you ready to let a big fish swim on? Because I'm not. Moreno may have gotten away, but this one won't. I'll make sure."

Without another word, Ethan draped the suit over the

fence, stalked to Uncle Gordon's car and leaned back against the driver's side door, a stony look on his face, arms crossed over his chest.

Maggie grimaced. "I'm sorry you've been caught up in all this—Sarah, the intruders, the van and now this. Ethan hasn't forgiven himself for the boy's death. The family's tried to give him time to heal, but…"

"Maybe if he helps you get this guy, he'll be able to let himself move forward again. I'm praying for him."

"I wish I hadn't had to call him in. But we don't have the experience for this kind of thing in the Loganton PD."

"He shouldn't waste his training and experience."

"You're right. And Loganton can sure use him." Maggie's chuckle lacked humor. "Hey, even you did better than we did. Want a job?"

"Don't be so hard on yourself. A uniform can put people off. And Carla struck me as the kind who doesn't like much scrutiny."

Maggie chuckled. "Maybe I should schedule a standing appointment at Monique's. I might get more info that way than by using police procedure."

Tess laughed. "It couldn't hurt."

As she unzipped her baggy protective splash suit, a vehicle approached, this one with the county sheriff's office seal on the side.

"Great," Maggie muttered. "Yet another layer to deal with." She turned to Ethan. "Go ahead and get out of here. Sheriff Benson might not take your presence as well as the chief does. He'll want to talk to both of you, but you might as well be comfortable when he hits you up."

Tess gave Maggie her protective gear, joined Ethan in the blue Cadillac and they drove away. With a glance out the back window, she saw the tall, khaki-uniformed sheriff staring after them, fists on his hips. She shivered.

"You can count on a visit from that guy," she told Ethan. "He doesn't look like the kind who'd take a meth lab in his county lightly."

"Good."

Tess slanted him a glance. He'd reverted to the marblelike rigidity she'd come to associate with the memories of his past. Her heart swelled with emotion, sympathy, a desire to comfort him and share his pain.

She had to admire a man willing to help her in spite of his painful memories and the career he'd felt he had to leave behind. Ethan had stepped into his nightmares to help her end hers.

She wished he would let the Lord heal his pain.

Tess had felt the urge to comfort Ethan before, but she hadn't known him, not well enough. And even though they'd only met a short time ago, because of what they'd shared, she now felt closer to him than to anyone else.

This time the urge to comfort him became need; this time she didn't hold back. She placed a hand on his forearm.

"I'm sorry you went through that horrible night a year ago," she said, her voice soft and gentle. "But you let it bring your life to a stop. I know helping me is the last thing you wanted to do, and may be one of the hardest things you've ever done."

The glance he sent her held no encouragement. But since she'd started down this path, she couldn't turn back. Tess breathed a quick prayer and went on, speaking from the heart.

"You've only told me a few details of what took place, but getting to know you has shown me more." She drew a breath for courage. "It might be hard for you to accept, but you weren't at fault back then—that drug dealer, Moreno, was. And you don't have to take on my problems to make up for the past. God knew your heart back then, and He knows it now, too."

He responded with a curt nod.

Tess added, "I want you to know how much I appreciate everything you've done, everything you're doing. And that I'm praying for you."

They didn't speak another word the rest of the way.

When had he given Tess such a clear look at his inner demons? How had he failed to see how perceptive she was?

He'd liked her from the start, even when he'd feared she might be involved. If he were honest with himself, something he always tried to be, he'd wanted her to be as innocent as she'd appeared.

Nothing like this had ever happened to him. He'd never met anyone like Tess before. She'd made him smile when little else had managed to pierce through the haze of pain.

And yet, he'd already failed her once. The van had struck.

At the hospital, he'd been unable to leave her side for more than brief periods at a time. He'd tried to tell himself a time or two that he'd do the same for anyone else, but he had to stop fooling himself.

He cared for Tess.

Even so, when had he let his guard down so much that she had come to know him so well?

The answer escaped him. But he couldn't deny the truth. She knew him better than Maggie, maybe even better than he knew himself. He'd never once voiced his guilty feelings over Robby's death. He hadn't wanted to acknowledge those emotions, to give them greater strength. Now Tess had zeroed in on them with stunning accuracy.

He'd failed Robby.

He'd failed Tess.

He might fail her again.

If a stranger's death had come so close to destroying him, what might the loss of Tess do?

He had two choices: he could fight or he could run.

He scoffed. Two choices? He only had one.

He had to get to whoever was after Tess.

Her life depended on it.

He was ready to do whatever it took to keep her safe.

At the Graver house, Ethan parked the car in the garage that opened to the alley in the rear. He and Tess got out, still silent, and the silence, while not comfortable, didn't weigh heavily on him.

The urgency of the situation, however, did.

As they walked through the backyard, he stayed on

full alert. Although he glanced at Tess a couple of times, he also scanned the shrubs on either edge of the property and made sure nothing hid in the shadows over the back stoop. When satisfied no danger to Tess lurked in the yard, he slanted her another look. On impulse, and before he could give himself the time to think it through, he reached out a hand.

No split-rail fence for an excuse this time.

She paused, then, meeting his gaze, laced her fingers through his, and they climbed the back steps side by side. He released her hand only so she could dig through her purse for the key.

In the kitchen Tess came to a full stop. "That drawer's not shut."

"What do you mean?"

"Uncle Gordon's a neat freak. He'd never leave the kitchen without making sure everything was just so."

At any other time he wouldn't give an open drawer a second thought, but after break-ins and murderous vans…he wanted to make sure.

"We were here after Mr. Graver and Miss Tabitha left," he said. "You didn't open it—"

"Ethan!" Impatience vibrated in her voice. "I didn't come into the kitchen. Remember? We stayed in the foyer and then stopped by my office to look at my listings."

"So an open drawer—"

"Something's wrong." Her eyes blazed. "I can feel it."

Before he could check for an intruder, secure the house, she ran into the hall. He followed on her heels.

In the foyer Tess stopped. Her eyes flew from the

console table to the grandfather clock; from the round green and tan rug to the graceful stairs; from the doorways to the living room and the sunroom.

"Aha!" She ran to her desk. "Someone *has* been here, Ethan. Look."

He glanced at the desk, then scanned the rest of the room. "Sorry, Tess. You'll have to show me. I don't see anything wrong."

"Don't you remember? We came in, I checked my listings, *closed my laptop* and then we left. Look again."

The laptop wasn't fully closed.

Ethan thought back. He remembered the *click* as it latched shut. "Your uncle—"

"Uncle Gordon thinks computers are boxes with letters and they suck the smarts out of people's brains. He'd never touch my laptop."

He reached for his phone, but before he dialed, he glanced at Tess. Color had drained from her face, and white edged her clamped lips. He wanted to wrap his arms around her and make things right for her.

Even more, he wanted to free her from the fear.

To do that, he really had to set aside his pain, to leave the past behind and reach forward, placing his trust in God, as she'd said. As he stared at Tess, Ethan realized he hadn't trusted God, not fully, with the outcome for a long time.

He was going to have to do just that.

It was going to take all his faith.

Forward, reach forward.

"Who has keys to the house?" he asked, his voice rougher than normal.

Her eyes widened. She gave him a brisk nod. "Uncle Gordon, Miss Tabitha, me and you—or did you give back the one Uncle Gordon loaned you? But that's it."

"I gave it right back. So three or four, and all accounted for—I hope." He dialed, waited and then his former partner picked up.

"Steven Kelly here."

Ethan couldn't help a smile. "Hey, it's Ethan."

"Hey, there, country boy! How're they treating you down there?"

Steve's booming voice matched his massive frame and fiery red hair. Even after Moreno's bullet, lodged too close to the spine to remove, had forced Steve into a wheelchair, his exuberance hadn't dimmed a watt.

With a pang Ethan realized how much he missed his friend. "They're okay, but they can't match you."

"Come back and hang out with me again. You know the agency will snap you back up and put you out on the street as soon as you say the word."

To Ethan's surprise, the sharp pang of emotion he'd felt every time he talked to Steve after the bust gone bad failed to occur. "Maybe I'll come visit soon. Right now, though, I need your help."

Even over the phone, Ethan knew when Steve went from friend to pro. "What's wrong?"

"You tell me."

"Know of any booming empires headed this way?"

"His or any of the others we—you—have on the books?"

"Nothing in particular, but I can check and let you know."

"How about..." Ethan couldn't believe he'd forgotten Moreno's accomplice's name.

"Alvarez? Nothing's happening with Alvarez. He's zipped his lips and is still in protective custody. We want him alive for trial, and to give Moreno inspiration to come out of hiding and try and shut him up. But Moreno knows we want him bad, that we'll jump on him the minute he shows his face. So he hasn't. We figure he's moved on. What's up with you?"

"This guy could be a lone ranger, but he also could be connected." Ethan brought Steve up to speed.

"I'm assuming," Steve said when Ethan was done, "you've called the agency in Charlotte."

"Maggie's doing a good job. Haz-Mat team's out at the site, the agency's sending folks, the sheriff just showed up and the whole PD's on the case."

"I'll overnight copies of some files—including Moreno's—to Charlotte. You'll have them tomorrow by three. I don't know that you'll find anything, but you sure are welcome to look." Then Steve fell silent.

Unease swirled in Ethan's gut. "Your turn. What's up?"

Steve's silence made the unease tighten to fear; Steve wasn't the kind to hold back. Finally, after clearing his throat, Steve said, "Word on the street is Moreno put you at the top of his most-wanted list last year. I wouldn't have said a thing, but since you're investigating this dealer, you need to know. It's not good enough for the PD to keep an eye on you anymore. I suspect Moreno's not the only one who knows about you by now. You messed up a great territory here in Chi-town. Whoever's down there won't want you around."

Before Ethan could voice his outrage over the Loganton PD keeping an eye on him without his knowledge, Steve went on.

"It's time you got your game back on. It's time for the real Ethan Rogers to please stand up."

TWELVE

Tess sensed a change in Ethan. Whatever his partner said had angered him—she'd come to know that particular narrowing of his eyes and tightening of his lips. But then he'd hung up and turned to her, nervous tension in his squared shoulders and his firm grip on her hand.

He led her from the office to the kitchen again.

Just then, Miss Tabitha and Uncle Gordon walked in from the film at the senior center.

"No, no," Miss Tabitha said when Tess gave her a quick hug. "I can't stay. I have to hurry home to thaw a large container of sauce and put water to boil for pasta. I have to feed my boarders."

So Tess, Uncle Gordon and Ethan dined on cooking school leftovers.

"That was great," Ethan said, standing. He took his plate, silverware and iced-tea glass to the sink, where he turned on the tap and squirted citrus-scented detergent on the dishes.

"You don't have to do that!" Tess cleared her place

and Uncle Gordon's, then hurried to Ethan's side. "I can take care of the cleanup."

He shrugged. "It's not a big deal. If I scrub and you dry and put away, we'll be done sooner."

As Tess stored the pan the class had used to bake the chicken-and-spinach lasagne, Ethan wiped down the table and countertops. Tess put the teakettle on to boil, set a mug, teabags and honey pot on the table, then went to her office for pens and a yellow legal pad. She and Ethan had agreed to take inventory of what they knew. The kitchen table was the perfect place to work.

Armed with her cup of Earl Grey, Tess sat to wait while Ethan helped Uncle Gordon up the stairs and into bed. For the first time since the break-ins, the house felt at peace. The blue-and-white kitchen, with its striped curtains, blue crockery, white cabinets and blue knobs soothed her frazzled nerves. Aged beams in the heart of the house creaked out their distinctive, familiar song.

Ethan returned. "Ready?"

Tess patted the yellow legal pad and pen in the center of the table. "Did you ask him about the keys?"

"And Miss Tabitha. All four are accounted for." Ethan took a seat across from Tess. "He also gave me a list of everyone who's been inside the house since you brought him home from the hospital. Why don't you make a list of everyone you remember?"

"You want to see if the lists match up."

"I don't think much gets by your uncle, but you've both been in and out at different times, and I want to know *everyone* who's had access to this house."

Tess thought through every day since she returned to Loganton. "Well, there's Uncle Gordon, Miss Tabitha and me." She jotted down the names. "You. All the cooking class students."

Ethan grinned and pretended to polish his nails on his shirt. "I asked your uncle their names. They're Ann Noonan, the knitting lady, Coach Moore and Nick Silvestre, newly retired."

Tess rolled her eyes and then had to scribble fast to catch up. "Who else?" she asked. "Who else—oh! Your friend Joe was here to fix the window and help you build the ramp. Your cousin and the rest of the PD have been in and out a couple of times, too, but they don't count, do they?"

He gave her a noncommittal look. "Anybody else?"

Tess thought and thought, then tapped her forehead between her eyes. "Of course! How could I forget? Stan the computer man's been here twice."

Ethan tapped the pad. "And you'd better add Mason Cutler to our list. Your uncle says his buddy came to see how he was getting along, and they wound up playing a game of chess."

"And argued no less than three times during the game."

Ethan chuckled. "He did say something about Mason's resemblance to a mule." He spun the legal pad so he could read the names. "He also said Art Reams stopped by, but I think we're on solid ground if we leave his name out."

"Here." Tess handed him a pen. "Start crossing off names. You know Uncle Gordon, Miss Tabitha—"

"I know."

His smile warmed every corner of Tess's heart. She wished she could freeze the moment. Having spent the better part of three weeks under suspicion of theft at her former employer, trust meant a great deal to her. Ethan had just given her a gift; his earlier suspicions were all gone.

After every awful thing that had happened to her, this quiet evening, their easy companionship and his welcome trust moved Tess to tears. She surreptitiously dabbed the corners of her eyes before Ethan noticed.

By the time he finished crossing off the most obvious names, she was able to smile back. Then he spun the notebook so it faced Tess.

"What do you think?" he asked. "Does that look right to you?"

She nodded.

"Then it looks like we're left with the cooking school students, Stan the computer man, Mason and Joe."

"You can take Mason off the list," Tess said. "He walks with a cane, and I doubt he could pull a four-leaf clover, much less an azalea or a rosebush."

A line went through Mason's name. Ethan tapped the next name with the tip of the pen. "Joe's about as decent as they come." Another line.

"No argument there," Tess murmured, studying the remaining names. "Okay. We have Coach Moore, Ann Noonan, Nick Silvestre and Stan."

"That's where I'll start tomorrow—"

"Where *we'll* start tomorrow."

Ethan met her gaze. "Wherever I can include you, I will. But when it's a matter of official business, my hands are tied."

Tess sighed. "Fair enough. I won't make things harder for you."

Ethan pushed away from the table. "Thank you, ma'am," he said in a teasing voice.

She joined him in the hall. "Much obliged, kind sir."

They walked to the foyer in comfortable silence. At the door she turned to Ethan. "Thanks."

His deep-blue eyes widened in surprise. "Thanks? What did I do?"

Where did she start?

She gestured toward the kitchen. "You gave me a peaceful evening in the middle of the nightmare my life's become."

Confusion drew parallel perpendicular lines between his brows. "We were narrowing down a list of suspects. How's that equal peaceful?"

"Okay, you're right. We were trying to figure out who might be responsible for all that's been happening, but I wasn't scared. And I knew I was safe with you."

"Don't give me more credit than I deserve."

"I didn't. When your house is invaded, when you've been shot at and when a madman's tried to turn you into roadkill…well, a moment of peace means a lot."

Ethan reached out and took her hand. Warm currents sped up her arm and through her. "With the Lord's help, I intend to put an end to the crime spree."

Well aware of the scars he bore, Tess tightened her

hold on his hand and looked into his beautiful blue eyes. "I trust you."

As she watched, Ethan's blue eyes glossed over with a damp sheen of emotion. "I promise to do everything in my power to keep you safe." He paused, swallowed hard. "Pray for me."

His raw honesty melted her heart. "I do, Ethan. I have, from the start."

He drew her closer. "My turn to say thanks."

His nearness sent ripples of delight straight to her head. The foyer seemed filled with a shimmering glow, and Tess wished she could freeze the moment in time. Her cheeks grew warmer. "You're welcome…"

His gaze still fixed on hers, and with deliberate gentleness, Ethan tipped up her chin with an index finger, then leaned down and pressed his lips to hers. Warmth and tenderness filled her. Her knees weakened, her head spun and her heart soared, full of joy.

With the same smooth motions, Ethan ended the kiss and stepped back. Their gazes clung until he turned, opened the door and walked away.

Tess locked up, leaned against the closed door. She wrapped her arms around herself, but couldn't bring back the warmth she'd felt. But the kiss…

With a dreamy smile, she spun in the middle of the foyer, giddy, her emotions in a whirl, logic gone, the magic of the moment she and Ethan shared like a hidden treasure in her heart.

Ethan's kiss…

That kiss warmed Tess's lips all night long.

* * *

The groundbreaking for the new community building at church was scheduled for late in the afternoon. Uncle Gordon and Miss Tabitha had gone into a cooking flurry. A row of treats now lined the dining room table, and Kiwi was a new fixture in the kitchen, unable to ignore the many delectable scents.

Ethan had called earlier to tell Tess he'd be spending most of the day with the agents from Charlotte. They would pore over files Steve had sent and plan future steps. He'd call her again once they finished. Otherwise, he planned to meet her at church.

Tess tried to focus on her listings, but too much had happened since she'd launched her business; it had dropped in her list of priorities. Eventually she made herself pack the two urns she'd sold, box her uncle's keychain collection, seal the microwave in its original box and head for the post office.

But the events of her recent past had turned something as simple as mailing packages into a frightening expedition. On her way to the garage with her wares, Tess peered at every shrub, weighed the danger in every shadow and questioned the safety of her own backyard.

The line at the post office crept at glacial speed, which gave her the opportunity to check out every man's hair color, shoulder breadth and whether she considered him short or tall.

Back home she parked on the street, scrambled out of the car, ran up the ramp and slammed the door shut. Then she settled in to wait...and wait. Patience didn't

figure prominently in Tess's list of virtues. She wanted
to know what Ethan had learned, but there was nothing
she could do until he gave her a call.

Soon enough, Tess showered, dressed in a butter-
yellow summer dress, and twisted her hair into a sleek
knot at the nape of her neck. She settled Kiwi in for the
night, shutting him in her office. Then she grabbed a
white linen jacket just in case the evening grew cold
and headed downstairs. Miss Tabitha was waiting for
Tess and Uncle Gordon; they'd agreed to drive to
church together.

Uncle Gordon maneuvered down the ramp with im-
pressive dexterity. By the time Tess had loaded the
bounty from the Graver kitchen into the car, he was
sitting in the front passenger seat, seat belt on, his folded
walker propped against the front bumper. Tess stowed
the contraption in the back seat, picked up Miss Tabitha
and, minutes later, got them to the church.

At first Tess was able to relax. The groundbreaking
ceremony went well, and dozens of people came to tell
her how pleased they were to see her again and how
sorry they were to hear of her troubles. She didn't know
where she found them, but she came up with endless
changes of topic.

Although the familiarity of her surroundings served
to soothe her anxiety for a while, when the early-
evening light outside the windows began to dim and
Ethan still hadn't arrived, a knot formed in Tess's
stomach and her head began to pound.

Could they possibly still be hashing out the ins and outs

of the case? Had something else come up? Maggie Lowe, a regular at church, hadn't put in an appearance, either.

"Tessie, girl!" Uncle Gordon called. He stood behind the multitable spread, a green apron snug around his slender frame. "Tabby forgot the spatula for the weiner schnitzel and a whole bunch of other stuff in the car. We've so much food here that all the utensils from the church's kitchen are out here already. Would you mind getting the brown bag in the trunk for us?"

Aha! Something to do. "Be right back."

Tess slipped outside, glad for the chance to hear herself think. The sun hovered on the edge of the horizon, and the sky in the west glowed a golden red. God's beauty never failed to amaze her.

"Father, You know why Ethan hasn't shown up. Protect him, and give me an extra measure of Your peace. Help me wait, help me trust—"

"Prayer don't help." Cold metal pressed the vulnerable spot behind her ear. "I want what is mine."

Father, help! Willing away a second shudder, Tess refused to let her assailant see her fear. "I don't know what you want. Tell me. I'll be happy to give it back. But unless I know what you want, I think—"

"Don't think." The metal prodded. "Move."

Tess took a step.

"No! This way."

Tess's captor nudged her toward the left where the heavy equipment was parked for the work scheduled to start the next day. She stumbled, then righted herself. "Just tell me where you want me to go. You don't have to push."

"To your car."

"There's nothing in the car but a bag full of kitchen gadgets."

"We go for drive."

"I don't have my keys."

He gave a metal jangle. "I have copy."

She couldn't get into that car. As long as they stayed in the parking lot, she could delay him until someone came outside and she could get help.

He nudged with his gun.

She balked.

He held Kiwi's carrier just within her line of vision. "You want the dog?"

She lunged. "Don't hurt him!"

He dropped the carrier with a thud and grabbed her arm. "You give me what is mine. Then you can have your dog."

The wrenching pain from his rough grip made her moan, but at least Kiwi was no longer in Tess's captor's grasp. If she could only figure out a way to distract him, maybe she could make him drop the gun—

Who was she kidding? She wasn't some Hollywood starlet in the latest blood-and-guts film. She could no more disarm the man than she could fly. Tess tried to remember everything she'd ever heard about self-defense.

And then it struck her—Kiwi hadn't made a sound. Had Joe hurt her dog? "Where is Ethan?" the creep whispered.

The man's voice resonated in her memory. She'd heard him before, and not just over the phone. Where? How? When had she heard this man? *Think, Tess, think!*

But too many thoughts eddied through her head.

Images clicked in and out of focus. Remembered sounds thundered in her ears. Fear like a river of ice ran through her veins.

"Ethan's on his way here," she answered, more frightened than she'd ever been, even more scared than when he bore down on her with the black van. And this time, she had an innocent dog to think about. "With his cousin and other law-enforcement personnel."

Her captor's nasty laugh grated against her left ear; the gun pressed tight against her right. She couldn't turn to either side or glimpse his face.

A sense of the surreal enveloped Tess. As if she'd been a spectator, her awareness grew keen. She noticed the backhoe parked behind the church, ready for tomorrow's work. She noticed the full parking lot and Pastor Reams's prized yellow bus. She again noticed Kiwi's unusual silence.

"What have you done to my dog?"

"Give me what I want, and you will know."

Tess's stomach turned, and in the waning light, despite the weird detachment fear had brought, she squinted, trying to look inside the carrier, to see the little dog. But it was dark enough by now that she couldn't make out his shape.

Could her captor be bluffing? Dare she test him?

The gun pressed tighter against her ear, but he didn't speak. He seemed unsure of his next step. Could she capitalize on his hesitance?

What could she do?

They'd reached an impasse. He wanted…whatever,

but refused to tell her what it was. She had no idea what he wanted, and couldn't convince him of that.

What now, Lord?

"We drive to your house."

If only she could distract him. There was no way she was getting into the car with this creep. "Not without my dog."

He muttered, and Tess couldn't catch what he'd said. "Slow," he said. "Slowly get the dog."

Tess moved inch by inch, his one hand tight on her left arm, the gun still at her ear. He moved with her, a terrifying bulk at her back. In what felt like slow motion, she leaned over and took hold of Kiwi's carrier.

She crashed down through the surreal, through the otherworldly sense of time. "He's not moving!" she cried, angry. In the dark, she reached for the upper tab. "Did you kill him?"

"Forget the dog. Drive to your house. You will find out there."

Then she knew, and her anger turned to fury. As she walked toward the Cadillac, the still Kiwi held close to her chest, Tess realized she wasn't going to be able to avoid getting in it. She also realized where she had heard the voice before.

"You don't want to do this, Joe," she said, starting the car. "Please put down the gun."

THIRTEEN

"There's little more in the file today than there was last year," Ethan told his cousin on their way to the church the next evening. They'd spent all day with the sheriff and the agency guys, staring at notes, studying photos, analyzing every last detail in the stack of files Steve had sent. When everyone complained of overload, they'd called it quits and agreed to meet again the next day.

At the red light, Ethan's fingers tapped out an uneasy beat on the steering wheel. "Steve didn't think we'd find anything conclusive."

Maggie didn't answer right away. Ethan looked at her out the corner of his eye. Her face revealed her doubts.

"I think," she said, "we have a drug problem in town. I also think it goes further than Sarah McVee and the vagrant who died late January and Kurt Minor, the teen who succumbed last fall. But I'm not convinced we're dealing with any of your big guys."

"Why not?"

"Because we're too small potatoes for them."

Ethan snorted. "There's no such thing as too small

for drug lords like Moreno. Loganton is the perfect place for a lab, especially since I'm sure Charlotte's quite a trophy for whoever gets his operation to beat out the competitors."

And me.

Maggie turned in her seat. "If Moreno's anywhere around here, it's more likely he's after you than trying to set up a new base of operations. You're the only one who saw him, and can place him in that alley." She gestured widely. "Here in Loganton our perp has gone after Tess, not you. Our problem has to do with Sarah, her death and the burned lab. I think our perp is homegrown."

He pulled into the church lot and parked behind the yellow school bus Art had bought for the youth group two months before. "One thing's for sure. We're not going to find Moreno or our perp here. I doubt either one's been near a church in years."

"We can agree on that."

As Ethan locked the SUV, the last touches of lavender faded into dark Prussian blue on the horizon. He couldn't believe they'd spent so long going over every bit of material he'd studied for two long years. Nothing new had jumped out at him.

Still, he couldn't shake the feeling Moreno was near. And he hated to think that it was all in his head. He didn't want Moreno to have so much power over him.

He wouldn't let a monster steal every second of his life. There would be enough time to deal with tomorrow's troubles when the sun rose again. With every ounce of determination he could summon, he set thoughts of the investigation aside. For the next few hours he was determined to pretend things were the way they'd been the day before Tess came back to town—with the added blessing of Tess's company.

"Ethan!" Gordon Graver called as the two cousins made their way through the clusters of church members. "Over here."

The waving spoon in Mr. Graver's hand reminded Ethan he'd only had a skimpy sandwich at noon. His stomach growled. He smiled and hurried to the table buried in platters and pans filled with delectable treats.

"What's good to eat—"

"Forget the food, boy," the older man said, his eyes panicked, his face pale. At his side Miss Tabitha wrung her hands.

Adrenaline rushed through Ethan's veins. "What's wrong?"

"Tessie's missing! She went out to the car to get a spatula an hour ago, and she hasn't come back."

On the surface Tess's delay in returning shouldn't alarm him. "She could have stopped to talk to someone. Look at all these people crammed into this small basement."

Gordon Graver shook his head, tears in his eyes, his lips trembling. "She wouldn't do that. She knew we needed more serving pieces. She's the kind who would talk after she brought 'em to us."

Ethan's heart pounded. "Did anyone go look for her?"

"Yes," Mr. Graver replied. "Art got all the men together. The parking lot lights had just gone on. There's no sign of her, and my car's gone, too."

"Did anyone call her cell phone?"

Mr. Graver held out his device. "Look."

In the past fifteen minutes he'd placed thirty-three calls to Tess. Ethan looked up, a knot in his gut.

"Go find my girl, son. She's all I got."

Ethan nodded. *Lord Jesus, spread your protection over her. Don't let me fail. Not this time.* "I'm on my way."

Where? Ethan didn't know. He just knew he would move mountains to find Tess.

"And pray," he added. "I'll be praying every step of the way."

Tess didn't know how she managed to guide the car in a straight line. Waves of shudders threatened, and bits of thoughts and partial prayers mingled in her head, but with gritted teeth she fought for the calm she'd need if she were to have any hope of survival. She couldn't give in to fear. She had to trust. God was in control, and Ethan was an experienced DEA agent.

Lord Jesus, Lord Jesus, Lord Jesus...

Unable to string together a coherent prayer, she kept her foot on the gas pedal, her hands on the steering wheel and her gaze on the road. The hopefully only drugged Kiwi in his carrier sat on the seat between them, while from the passenger seat Miss Tabitha's boarder held his gun aimed at her head.

To keep her mind from dwelling on her horrific situation, Tess corralled her thoughts and concentrated on Ethan. She couldn't imagine how he'd feel when he realized his buddy was behind the attacks. She lifted him in prayer.

As she applied the brakes for the red light, she slanted Joe a sideways look. Then, in spite of her abductor's narrowed eyes and steady stare, she saw him chew the inside of his lip. One of Tess's co-workers in Charlotte had done the same thing when under extreme stress.

After another silent prayer, she took a deep breath. "Why would you kill Sarah? Didn't you make money selling her the drugs?"

Joe's expression turned vicious, and the gun came closer. "Shut up! Drive faster."

"Did she owe you money? Is that why you met in the woods? Didn't she pay for her drugs?"

The light turned green. Tess pressed the gas pedal and out of the corner of her eye, saw the gun waver the tiniest bit. Had she not been so keen on unsettling him, she wouldn't have noticed. Clearly Joe felt Sarah had done him wrong.

Father, show me...guide me... "How about this?" she said. "Did Sarah set herself up in business with your goods? Did she cheat you? Did she skim profits or keep a little of the goods back, then sell them and pocket the dough?"

She grimaced. No one would buy her impression of a 1920s gun moll. *Hurry, Ethan!*

Whether Tess's lousy act was responsible or not, Joe squirmed as she pulled up to the house. "No!" he said in the harsh whisper she now knew too well. "Park in the alley. In the back."

Though he was evil, he wasn't stupid. Tess might stand a chance if she could slow him down in front of the house where neighbors might take a walk or a car might drive by. In the alley?

It was usually deserted.

Still, she had no choice. She did as he demanded. Behind the garage, she put the car in neutral and faced her abductor. "What do you want now? You've got the gun, so you're calling the shots. But I'll tell you, I don't have a key to the house or the garage."

He pulled a key chain from his pocket and tossed it on her lap. "Park here. Use my keys."

Her courage wavered. He'd had copies made of all their keys. No wonder he'd had such free access. He must have somehow made a mold of the keyholes with either putty or gum. No one had thought anything of his coming and going while he worked with Ethan on the ramp. They'd trusted him.

Chills racked her.

A verse from the book of Psalms floated to her mind. It reminded her to be strong and let her heart take courage and wait for the Lord.

After a deep, calming breath, Tess turned off the car. Before she could pocket the keys, Joe snatched them from her. Her index finger got caught on the key chain, and his rough handling bent the finger back to an awkward angle. Pain sizzled up her arm. Tess moaned.

"Shut up," Joe hissed. "Get out now. We'll go find it."

Panting from the pain, Tess used her good hand to open the car door. She grabbed Kiwi's soft fabric carrier, hugged it close, stepped out and stood on shaky legs. As she squared her shoulders, she mouthed the verse again and came to a decision. If she only had a few minutes of life left, she wanted to know why she was going to die.

"Look, Joe," she said in a calm, even voice. "You want something Sarah took from you, either money or drugs, I don't know which. But I don't have it, whatever it is. I didn't even know her, so you're making a mistake." Tess raised Kiwi's carrier to within inches of Joe's face. "This is sick. You've used an innocent dog. Let me go take care of him and turn yourself in. You still have the chance to change your life—"

"Dog, dog! Stop whining about the stupid *dog!*" He swatted at the carrier. It snagged on the gun. He tugged.

Tess pulled.

He yanked.

"Give me back my dog—"

With a tearing sound the carrier ripped, Tess screamed with every cell in her body. "Help! Help, help, help me, please—"

He backhanded her mouth, and Tess groaned at the shock. Her teeth cut through the soft tissue of her lips. Blood oozed; she spit, then gritted her teeth to keep from moaning in pain, bracing against another blow from the enraged man.

When the blow never came, she opened her eyes to look at Joe. Then she saw what had distracted him. From between the shredded edges of the colorful fabric carrier, over her arm as she held it close, small lumps of whitish crystals dropped on the blacktop surface of the alley. Although she'd never seen methamphetamine in any form, she knew what the cascade meant.

Now that Joe had found his missing goods, Tess and Kiwi had lost all value. He looked up, met her gaze. Then he raised the gun even with her eyes.

Out in the church parking lot, Maggie used her phone to mobilize the PD and notify the sheriff's office, while Ethan called in the Charlotte DEA agents on his device. They needed all the help they could get.

Then he tried Tess's number again; she still didn't answer.

When her voice mail came on, Ethan slapped his cell phone shut. He caught snippets of his cousin's terse conversation. "Yes, sir...all roads in or out sealed...guard at the Graver home...surrounding counties...doubt he'll leave town, but we'll cover all bases."

"I'm taking Mr. Graver home," he said when she hung up. "Will the guard be there?"

"Wayne's on his way. I don't have a better man to trust with Mr. Graver's safety."

Ethan nodded and started toward his SUV. Maggie called his name. He shot a glance over his shoulder. He kept walking; he couldn't stand to waste a second more. Tess was in danger.

"We'll find her," his cousin said.

"I pray it's in time."

"Amen!"

They hurried off, Ethan to collect Mr. Graver, and

Maggie to question the people still gathered in the basement.

"Any word?" Gordon Graver asked the minute he spotted Ethan.

"Not yet, but we're on it, sir."

The older gentleman lowered his gaze to his hands, tight on his shiny walker. Ethan watched his lips move silently, and he reached out to cover the thin, aged hand with his.

"Father God," he said, his voice low, his plea heartfelt. "You know where Tess is. Comfort and protect her, keep her safe. Guide us to where she's being held…"

After the men voiced their amens, Ethan walked Mr. Graver to the SUV, helped him up into the elevated vehicle, ran around the back and drove off.

At the Graver home, Ethan found Wayne Donelly pacing the length of the wide front porch.

The house was silent; even the dog didn't bark. Ethan hoped Mr. Graver would be able to keep Killer quiet once they went inside even though he didn't expect to find anything here.

"Are you alone?" he asked Wayne in a whisper.

The officer nodded. "Everyone else is out looking for her. You and I can handle the house. Are you armed?"

Ethan shook his head. "I don't think we'll find them here. This guy's been through the house enough times. I think he got desperate and snatched Tess. He hasn't found what he'd been looking for. Since you're armed, why don't you keep Mr. Graver with you while you check out the first floor?"

Wayne looked ready to argue but then gave a quick nod.

"Let's go," Mr. Graver urged in a raw, sibilant plea. "My girl's out there. The sooner you check the house, the sooner you'll be out looking for her again."

Wayne drew his weapon, aimed it at shoulder height and nodded for Mr. Graver to unlock the door.

The officer slipped inside as silent as a dancer. Experience showed, and Ethan felt a short-lived relief.

Until he could hold Tess again, he wouldn't relax.

Mr. Graver leaned his walker against a wall, and with surprising ease and grace, followed Ethan into the foyer, using his free hand to steady himself against the walls.

On silent feet, Ethan climbed the stairs, thankful for Mr. Graver's maintenance-mania, as Tess called it. The floorboards were solid.

The second-floor hall was empty. Four doors flanked it, and Ethan opened the first. It led to a large, white bathroom, empty, the window over the tub locked, nothing behind the old-gold curtains.

He moved on. The next door opened into a large bedroom, the double bed dressed in tan covers, a pile of turquoise and cream pillows piled against the headboard. The closet held only hangers, and the window here, too, was locked.

Across the hall Ethan walked into Gordon Graver's large, masculine room. The scent of a spicy aftershave immediately painted the older man's face in his mind's eye.

The handsome navy-and-gray-striped duvet on the antique mahogany bed hadn't been disturbed. Ethan crossed the silver-gray carpet to check behind the navy drapes on the tall windows on either side of the headboard. He found nothing there. A glance into the navy and white bathroom told him it, too, was empty.

Then, with a tremor in his fingers, he turned the old cut-glass doorknob on Tess's bedroom door. While spice had fragranced her uncle's bedroom, hers held the light scent of flowers he'd come to recognize as trademark Tess. Soft yellow walls and white trim gave the room a cheerful air, and gauzy green curtains only offered decoration to the window. They would never block the sun.

Green-on-green stripes ran the length of her bedcover, and Tess had left a pair of fuzzy white slippers at the foot of the bed.

Standing in a room that could belong to no one but Tess, his heart ached. *Father, protect her from all harm.*

There was no one in the house, at least, not on the second floor. On the main floor he checked in with Wayne, who stood in the foyer at Mr. Graver's side.

"Did you look downstairs?" Ethan asked.

The officer nodded. "I found a mountain of junk, but nothing else. No sign of Tess and no sign of a perp."

From somewhere outside, Ethan heard something, a muted yell, maybe more than one. *Tess!*

"Did you hear that?" he asked.

"What?" Wayne's eyes narrowed, his expression alert.

Ethan listened intently for a repeat of what he'd heard. Long, silent seconds passed. Not a sound. Maybe he'd imagined what he wanted to hear.

Ethan shook off his disappointment. "I don't hear it now."

"The house is clear," Wayne said. "Go ahead. I'm stuck here, but you should join the search."

"As soon as I know something—anything—Mr. Graver, I'll give you a call. Please pray. Lord willing, we'll find her soon."

Wayne and Tess's uncle nodded. Ethan strode to the door. *Lord willing...*

Did he trust God's will? Could he accept it, no matter what?

"Faith, Father," he prayed as he closed the front door. "Strengthen my faith."

As he ran to the SUV, his cell phone rang. "Hello?"

"Don't speak," a raspy male voice whispered. "Come to the alley for Tess."

Ethan froze. His thoughts tangled, and nothing made sense. His hand clenched around the phone. He took a deep breath, hoping for calm, but finding none. "Which alley?"

"Behind the yellow house, Mr. Graver's house."

Lord God...be with me. "I'll be right there."

With a glance over his shoulder and nausea in his throat, Ethan hurried around to the side yard, then measured his pace as he crossed to the back. He flipped open his phone again, dialed Maggie and prayed she'd answer. Voice mail picked up. He whispered a quick description of their situation, hoped his cousin understood what he'd said, that she'd check her messages soon. Then he hung up and walked ahead.

In the backyard, he paused. Tension knotted his shoulders; he rolled them to ease the twinge of pain in his neck. He cast a glance over a shoulder, surveyed the vegetation by the light of the slender new moon and only then realized his mistake.

He'd given the madman a perfect target. He hadn't thought to alert Wayne. It would have meant leaving Mr. Graver alone in the house, but they'd already checked it and found it clean. They could have locked him in.

Too late now.

Guilt swamped him. He should have kept his mind on the case, but his only thought had been of Tess. Now he had no weapon, and this man had used a gun on the two of them before. What did he expect to accomplish by running out here without even a plan?

His blunder might have put Tess in greater danger than before. What could he do?

Alone? Nothing.

With God? Only God knew.

Ethan bowed his head, frustration a living thing inside. *Oh, Father, I failed Tess again. She placed her trust in me, and I'm useless to her like this. I know it's all about faith, and I know trust is more than a word. But, Father, I can't do this alone. You can do anything. I need Your wisdom and Your strength. Help me, Father, help me help her. In Jesus' name, amen.*

"Okay," he called out. "I'm here. Where's Tess?"

"She's here. Come to the alley."

"No way. Send her out. If I see her, I'll come back."

His only response was Tess's moan. He took a step.

"Don't!" she cried. "He has what he wants—aaaah!"

Tess's second cry of pain hit Ethan in the heart. He

had to do whatever it took to save the woman he was coming to love. And maybe, maybe then God would give them a future to see where their feelings might lead.

Determined, he stepped in the direction from which Tess's cry had come. He moved up against the side of the double garage, careful not to misstep on the gravel walk around the structure. His breath sounded harsh and loud in his head. His heartbeat matched it. Could the madman hear him approach?

If he couldn't, maybe Ethan could distract him by throwing some of the rocks underfoot. Then Ethan would make his move. He prayed Tess wasn't injured and could respond, maybe run to safety, when he did.

I trust you, she'd said.

Ethan had placed his trust in God.

Clinging to faith, he reached down, felt among the pieces of gravel, found a relatively large one and straightened again. He scanned the yard for a target. Toward the back, about eighteen feet away, sat the Gravers' large, aluminum trashcans. With God's help and by His Grace, Ethan hoped to hit one on his first attempt.

Remembering years of Little League, he wound up, aimed and threw the rock. "I can do this through Christ…"

Claaang!

The noise startled Joe. It gave Tess the opportunity she'd been waiting for. She drew her arm forward, aimed and jammed her elbow into his ribs.

"Ooof!"

As he fought to regain his balance, Tess twisted away,

but Joe was too quick. He smashed the gun up against her head again.

Ethan appeared around the corner of the garage.

Tess knew the moment he discovered her abductor's identity. He drew a rough, shocked breath then whispered, "Joe," pain in his voice. "Why?"

"Get in car," Joe commanded. "Both of you. Now."

Ethan wavered. She met his gaze and winced at the betrayal she read there. Now more than ever she wished she could reach out and comfort him. But first they had to deal with Joe.

Then Ethan's gaze turned deadly, and Tess got a glimpse into the drug enforcement agent he'd once been. Shoulders squared, chin high, eyes blazing at Joe, he faced his former friend toe-to-toe.

"Why?" he asked. "Tell me, and I'll go with you."

Joe shrugged, unwilling or unable to hold that stare. "You know too much now. In the car."

"What? What do you think I know?" Ethan asked, clearly playing for time. "I have no idea why you took Tess. What is this all about?"

Although the gun Joe held to her head didn't waver, Tess realized why Ethan was asking the same question again. Joe answered, "You know. You're not stupid. You know too much."

"I thought you were my friend," Ethan continued.

Tess gave a minuscule nod, and then, determined to thwart Joe's murderous intent and ready to fight to the end, she dropped and punched the back of Joe's knee. It buckled, just as she'd hoped.

"Hey!" Joe howled.

"Duck!" Tess yelled.

The gun went off as Joe collapsed on top of her. Panic threatened. Tess couldn't budge. Her gaze darted everywhere, but all she could see was dark sky, white garage, blades of grass and Joe's back. She tried to breathe, but the weight on her chest made it impossible.

Then Ethan flew at his former friend, pushing him off. The two men grappled, wrestled and grunted. In the dark she made out the outline of tangled limbs. Tess rolled away, panting and waiting for the right moment to launch her body at them, to come to Ethan's aid.

A second shot rang out.

A man screamed.

Light flooded the yard as law-enforcement officials converged. Numb, Tess lay frozen in place, too frightened to move. Nausea roiled in her stomach. Her head throbbed. Then like a fool she began to cry.

She needed to know.

She couldn't bear to know.

Which man was shot?

For Tess, time flew by in a blur. Maggie's team had rushed up, clapped handcuffs on Joe, who'd refused to utter a word, and then cordoned off the Gravers' property. A pair of EMTs came to check on Tess, but she waved them away. "I'm fine. Help Ethan, please!"

Joe's bullet had pierced Ethan's chest, and the dark stain had grown larger by the second. "Please save his life," she'd cried.

By the time she got back to Kiwi, who she'd left behind the garage, the little dog had begun to rouse. Wayne offered to keep Kiwi until Tess came back home.

One of Maggie's fellow officers then drove the three of them, Uncle Gordon, Maggie and Tess to the hospital. They'd spent agonizing hours while doctors worked to stop the loss of blood, find the bullet and repair the damage it had wrought.

Miss Tabitha had joined them in the family waiting room, since her house was also cordoned off while the authorities gathered evidence. The four of them spent the hours in prayer while doctors worked to save Ethan's life. Random efforts at sleep proved futile.

At dawn Uncle Gordon and Miss Tabitha headed down to the hospital's cafeteria for a bite to eat. Both needed food for their various medications. Tess took advantage of their absence to grill Maggie for answers to the questions she still had.

"Sarah got herself in trouble with Joe when she started skimming meth to keep for herself," Tess said. "But I still don't understand what she used to do for Joe, since I suppose his 'government' job was just what he did for the Sanitation Department."

"From what we've managed to piece together," Maggie said, her eyes red-rimmed, her face pale, "she distributed the meth to three teen pushers. They were the ones selling at the high school."

Tess shuddered. "So she was as evil as Joe turned out to be."

"There are no good guys in the drug trade. When Joe

realized her addiction had grown to such an extent that she couldn't resist the temptation to steal more than the free supply he gave her as partial payment, he knew she had outlived her usefulness."

"It was murder, then."

"Without a doubt."

Tess caught her bottom lip between her teeth. "So Joe broke into our house looking for the meth he couldn't account for."

"And to make good use of your brand-new business."

"What? That doesn't make sense."

Maggie sighed. "He figured out the urns Miss Tabitha gave you to sell were the perfect containers for shipping the drug manufactured locally to dealers elsewhere."

"My laptop! That's why it kept crashing. What did he do to it?"

"Not much. He just kept you from following your transactions too closely. He and his contacts manipulated the sales to make sure they won the urns."

Tess slumped into her maroon-and-gray-striped armchair. "Oh, no! All that drug. I shipped them yesterday afternoon."

"The DEA took the laptop," Maggie said, a mild apology in her voice. "They're now ready to pick up the accomplices on the other end when the urns arrive in the mail. Your records had the addresses they needed."

Just then a green-garbed doctor entered the room. "You're waiting for Mr. Rogers?"

The two women leaped to their feet. "I'm his cousin," Maggie said.

Tess regretted having no claim. No claim, other than the love in her heart. Ethan had been willing to give up his life for her. Beyond all the reasons she'd found to love him, that had shown her more about his character than anything else.

"Well," the gray-haired surgeon said. "He's in rough shape, but we think he'll pull through. He's a lucky man. That bullet barely missed his heart."

"It wasn't luck," Tess whispered. "It was God."

The doctor rubbed his forehead. "Luck…God… doesn't matter which. It's going to be a while before you can see him, but he should be able to talk by tomorrow or the next day."

It matters! Tess hoped she'd have the opportunity to tell the doctor how much in the days to come. For now, it was enough to know her prayers for mercy had been answered.

"Thank you," she said, echoing Maggie's sentiments.

Time to turn to God in prayer again. This time for healing.

"Hey!"

Tess blinked at the softly uttered word. She'd fallen asleep in the chair next to Ethan's hospital bed after hours of watching for any response. Uncle Gordon and Miss Tabitha had agreed to go home once they'd heard the doctor's good news. Maggie had gone to the PD to finish paperwork related to the case. When she finished there, the two women had traded vigils in six-hour chunks.

"You're still here," Ethan whispered.

She leaned over the side rail, her heart singing with joy. "Where else would I be?"

He smiled. "Selling urns."

Tess shuddered. "I'm out of the urn business for good. Turns out, Joe filled the two I sold with meth. He fiddled with my listings to make sure his buddies won the auctions and I shipped them the drugs. Just for using me, I hope he spends the rest of his life behind bars."

"The laptop problems…"

"Yep. The laptop problems." Then she remembered something else, something to ease some of his fears. "Maggie says there's no evidence of Moreno's involvement. It seems Joe set up the meth lab to make extra money. He met Sarah when he sold her the meth, and it didn't take him long to figure out he could romance and woo her into doing anything he said. The two of them wreaked havoc here in town, and then he realized she was cutting into his profits by using more than he was willing to have her use. Then, when I came home and he realized what I was up to on the Internet, he figured he could use my business to ship out the drugs and expand."

He winced. "I thought we were friends…"

Oh, no! What had she done? "I'm sorry. I shouldn't have said anything. This isn't the time for any of that. We should be celebrating how well you're doing. There's plenty of time to talk about all *that*."

"It's okay," he said, his gaze sad. "I woke up a couple of hours ago. I thought a lot and prayed even more. I can't be looking for Moreno behind every tree. If I do, I won't have any life. It is all about trust in God."

"I'll remind you if you slip up," she said with a smile.

"I'll be counting on you," he replied seriously.

The warmth she'd come to associate with Ethan's touch filled her, and this time he'd done it with tender words, words with a world of promise. "We'll remind each other."

His nod was emphatic. "Joe's betrayal? It hurts. But lately I've learned a lot about the man I am. I'm also learning about the man God wants me to become." He tried to shrug but winced at the effort.

She reached for the nurse's bell. "Do you need something for the pain?"

"No, they have me full of more than enough junk. I'm just not used to being tied down like this. I'll be okay."

She studied his face, trying to fix in her mind every tiny detail. His dark, tousled hair, his beautiful blue eyes, his rare grin, even the stubble that darkened his chin were precious to her. The hours she'd spent at his side, praying for his life and his complete recovery, had shown her how deep her feelings had grown. They'd turned into love.

She'd do anything to spare him pain. "Are you sure?"

Ethan drew a deep breath. "Yeah. As long as I remember to trust God all the time, no matter what, I'll be fine." His eyelids fluttered, and Tess turned toward the chair again, sure he needed the sleep.

"Don't," he whispered. "Stay here with me."

Tess took hold of the hand he held out. "Aren't you sleepy?"

He shook his head. "I just want to spend time with you."

She smiled. "As long as you want."

One blue eye opened a crack. "That's something we're going to have to talk about, Tess."

"There's a lot I want to tell you."

The other blue eye opened to match the first. Ethan's slow smile held a hint of mischief. Tess's heart soared but she didn't dare say a word; it might erase his smile.

"I'm hoping," he said, his voice lighthearted, "that there'll be some show-and-tell to go with the talk."

Tess blushed, their kiss a vivid memory. "Oh…I suppose that could be arranged."

"How about starting now?"

"You're injured and in a hospital bed!"

"Doesn't mean I'm all washed up. Besides, a patient needs TLC."

"But…but…"

He arched a brow. "Wimp?"

Her eyes widened. "Not on your life, Mr. Agent Man!"

Before he could say another word, she lowered the side rail and leaned close.

"I love you," he whispered.

"I love you right back." And she kissed him on the lips.

EPILOGUE

Six weeks later, Tess twisted and turned in front of her vanity mirror, trying for a good look at all sides. Kiwi, none the worse for his drug-induced nap, sat in the middle of her bed, watching her every move. His fur looked less moth-eaten these days, but he'd never be a beauty. She loved him anyway.

He still hated Ethan.

"And that's why you're staying in here," she told her dog.

Ethan's recovery had been slow but steady. She'd spent as much time as possible with him each and every day. He'd muscled through hours of painful therapy, and was only now regaining range of motion in his left arm. Tess had helped him with his exercises, and they'd fallen deeply in love, at least, that was what she thought. He hadn't said that word again.

Now, they were on their way out to their first real date outside the hospital.

A final look in the mirror told her she looked good. The green-and-white summer dress helped the green flecks in her hazel eyes stand out, and her light tan looked richer against the soft colors. Strappy white sandals revealed the red polish Angie, the nail tech at Monique's, had applied to her toenails.

The doorbell rang. Tess's heart gave a little hitch.

"I'm coming!" And she ran down.

When she reached the midway point on the stairs, Ethan let out a wolf whistle. "You look great!" he said.

Kiwi barked like mad.

Tess's cheeks heated. "Umm…shouldn't we get going? We have at least an hour's drive."

With a wink, Ethan held open the door. "You just want to get me away from your pooch. I don't know why he hates me—unless he's plain old jealous."

As Tess walked past him, she glanced up, and with more daring than she'd thought she had, said, "Does he have reason for his jealousy?"

"What do you think?"

She wasn't *that* daring! So they walked to his SUV in silence. Once both were buckled, he turned on a classical CD and they returned to the easy conversation they always shared.

The restaurant was located in a century-old mansion, its many rooms converted into cozy dining rooms with no more than three small tables per room. Crystal chandeliers gleamed overhead, and in the middle of each table, crystal candelabra sparkled as well.

Rich, creamy linens dressed the tables. The luxury of upholstered chairs provided diners with sumptuous comfort.

Ethan kept the conversation flowing, and they both laughed repeatedly during the meal.

"Ready for dessert?" he asked.

"Are you kidding? I'm stuffed."

"Aw, come on! How often do we get the chance to eat like this? Maybe just a bowl of strawberries. I've heard this place is famous for them."

Tess resisted—for all of about three seconds. "Okay, but you might wind up eating most of them."

"What a hardship! A helping of my favorite fruit."

When the waiter, in his tux and crisp white shirt and tie, brought Tess the footed bowl full of berries, she groaned. "Too much…"

And then she saw it. The light from the chandeliers caught on it, making it twinkle like one of the prisms overhead.

Tess reached out a tentative finger.

"Go ahead," Ethan whispered.

All sound seemed to fade. The only things that registered with Tess were the man across the table from her and the diamond nestled among the fruit.

With shaking fingers, she touched the jewel. "Ethan…?"

"I love you, Tess. Will you marry me?"

Her tears flowed. She picked up the ring, handed it to her future husband and met his beautiful blue gaze. She held out her left hand.

Dear Reader,

Danger in a Small Town is the first in my *Carolina Justice* series. Yes, the books deal with justice, but they also deal with faith and the hope our faith brings us.

To reach that blessed hope, though, isn't easy—faith rarely is. A believer is called to trust a God he or she can't see or touch, but one who promises to always be at our side. That's where trust, the issue Tess and Ethan deal with, comes in. I've always seen this as one of the most difficult aspects of my faith. It's not hard to believe in the God who created everything I see around me; it's more difficult to trust God to be there for me when so many more complex and urgent issues can capture and hold His attention.

Jesus's ministry on earth is proof of God's love for each and every one of us, but the distance of time often lets us forget that truth. During times of forgetfulness, I turn to a favorite Scripture verse: "Be still, and know that I am God." To me, that's where the essence of faith lies, where we quit trying and start trusting that God is in control, where we find the peace God promises. I hope that, like Tess and Ethan, you can trust and find His peace.

Blessings,

QUESTIONS FOR DISCUSSION

1. Have you ever faced a difficult situation, one where you felt you could no longer be effective, and where the only option seemed to be to ditch everything and start fresh? Did you? Explain.

2. Have you ever had to care for an older relative who didn't feel he or she needed that care? How did you both handle the situation?

3. Crime seems to be everywhere today. Have you been a victim of a crime? How did your faith help you through?

4. Tess's every action was under scrutiny at work for a few weeks. In the end, she was innocent, but her coworkers couldn't get beyond their suspicions. Have you ever been unfairly accused? How did the people around you respond? Have you ever unfairly accused someone else of something?

5. Even though she is strongly attracted to Ethan, Tess doesn't want to put herself in the position of caring for someone who doesn't trust her. How would you have handled an attraction under her circumstances?

6. Ethan's memories of the bust-gone-wrong have altered his life drastically. Has there been any one

life event that has changed yours? Did you, like Ethan, run from that event? Or did you run to the change it brought?

7. After the bust, Ethan loses his ability to trust. He feels he failed Robby and his partner, and can't trust his training and experience. How do you view his response to the tragic event?

8. Tess reminds Ethan that Scripture calls a believer to leave the past behind and reach toward the future. Have you been able to forgive yourself and others for things in your past and head toward a faith-filled future? If not, how can you go about doing that?

9. When Ethan loses the ability to trust himself, is it really himself he's not trusting? What does that lack of trust say about a person's faith in God? How does your faith impact your view of your own abilities and gifts?

10. Joe betrayed Ethan's trust. This could have made Ethan revert to viewing the event as another failure on his part—not recognizing Joe as untrustworthy. Instead, he acknowledges his pain and his difficulty getting past it, but he doesn't blame himself. How would you have reacted in his place?

REQUEST YOUR FREE BOOKS!

2 FREE RIVETING INSPIRATIONAL NOVELS
PLUS 2 FREE MYSTERY GIFTS

Love Inspired®
SUSPENSE

YES! Please send me 2 FREE Love Inspired® Suspense novels and my 2 FREE mystery gifts (gifts are worth about $10). After receiving them, if I don't wish to receive any more books, I can return the shipping statement marked "cancel". If I don't cancel, I will receive 4 brand-new novels every month and be billed just $4.24 per book in the U.S. or $4.74 per book in Canada, plus 25¢ shipping and handling per book and applicable taxes, if any*. That's a savings of over 20% off the cover price! I understand that accepting the 2 free books and gifts places me under no obligation to buy anything. I can always return a shipment and cancel at any time. Even if I never buy another book, the two free books and gifts are mine to keep forever.

123 IDN ERXX   323 IDN ERXM

Name	(PLEASE PRINT)	
Address		Apt. #
City	State/Prov.	Zip/Postal Code

Signature (if under 18, a parent or guardian must sign)

Order online at www.LoveInspiredSuspense.com

Or mail to Steeple Hill Reader Service:

IN U.S.A.: P.O. Box 1867, Buffalo, NY 14240-1867
IN CANADA: P.O. Box 609, Fort Erie, Ontario L2A 5X3

Not valid to current subscribers of Love Inspired Suspense books.

Want to try two free books from another series?
Call 1-800-873-8635 or visit www.morefreebooks.com

* Terms and prices subject to change without notice. N.Y. residents add applicable sales tax. Canadian residents will be charged applicable provincial taxes and GST. This offer is limited to one order per household. All orders subject to approval. Credit or debit balances in a customer's account(s) may be offset by any other outstanding balance owed by or to the customer. Please allow 4 to 6 weeks for delivery. Offer available while quantities last.

Your Privacy: Steeple Hill Books is committed to protecting your privacy. Our Privacy Policy is available online at www.SteepleHill.com or upon request from the Reader Service. From time to time we make our lists of customers available to reputable third parties who may have a product or service of interest to you. If you would prefer we not share your name and address, please check here. ☐

LISUS08

Love Inspired.
HISTORICAL
INSPIRATIONAL HISTORICAL ROMANCE

An English gentleman by day, Matthew Covington becomes the mysterious crime-fighter Black Bandit at night—and nothing can tempt him to reveal his secret identity. Until he meets reporter Georgia Waterhouse, who shares his passion for justice. What will become of their growing love if he reveals the truth that lies behind the mask?

Look for

Masked by Moonlight

by

ALLIE PLEITER

Available June 2008 wherever you buy books.

Steeple Hill®

www.SteepleHill.com

Love Inspired SUSPENSE

TITLES AVAILABLE NEXT MONTH

Don't miss these four stories in June

BAYOU PARADOX by Robin Caroll

When a mysterious illness strikes down two women in Tara LeBlanc's life, she knows she's the one who will find the cause. By-the-book sheriff Bubba Theriot has his hands full trying to track down the suspects *and* keep Tara safe from the bayou, the culprits and her own dangerous instincts.

FINAL JUSTICE by Marta Perry
Reunion Revelations

The DNA test proves it: Mason Grant is a father. What's more, his nine-year-old daughter has been in the custody of her mother's killer all these years. With the help of old college friend Jennifer Pappas, Mason tries to adjust to fatherhood, but the killer isn't through with them yet.

KEEPING HER SAFE by Barbara Phinney

Hunter Gordon would have done anything for the Bentons—he'd even plead guilty to a crime he hadn't committed. Now that Rae Benton is in danger, Hunter is determined to keep her safe...if Rae will let him. But before he can help her, Hunter will have to win back her trust.

KILLER CARGO by Dana Mentink

Pilot Maria de Silva is shocked to find a hidden stash of drugs in the midst of the pet supplies she's delivering. Her only refuge in an unfamiliar town is Cy Sheridan's animal sanctuary. Can Cy protect her from the danger that lurks outside?

LISCNM050B